THE MYSTERY OF THE CRAZY QUILT

HARLAND CREEK MYSTERY QUILTERS

JODI ALLEN BRICE

To all my readers who love my mysteries. Petunia and I are grateful for you!

CHAPTER 1

I looked at the wall clock of the quilt shop and let out a groan.

Sighing, I stopped the long-arm quilter and walked out into the front of the quilt shop to find my mom ringing up another sale.

I waited until the customer left and shot Mom a look.

She glanced at me and shrugged. "Dove, I really don't think this snow is going to stick. Mississippi never gets snow, and when we do, it never sticks. There is no need to close early."

I narrowed my eyes. "Have you looked outside? It's coming down hard, and the temps are dropping. We don't want to be on the road when it ices. We need to get home."

Mom bit the corner of her lip. "I don't know. I've had the best sales day of the year. You know how people are when it gets bad weather. They like to come in and shop for material so they can quilt if they get stuck at home."

I crossed my arms. "Is another sale worth sliding off the road into a ditch on your way home? We need to get home while the roads are still travelable."

My mom's shoulders slumped, and I knew I had won the battle. "Fine. But I need to run this fabric over to Weenie's house before I go home. She was going to come by, but she seems to be running late. I'll phone her and tell her I'll drop it off, so she won't be out in this weather."

I brightened. "Perfect. I'll start shutting everything down." I headed to the back room and began turning off the lights and the sewing machines.

After gathering my purse, I slipped on my winter coat. I snuggled against the soft white wool and smiled as the fur-lined hood brushed against my skin. My mom had told me it was foolish to buy a white coat that would show every stain, but I didn't care. I had splurged and bought it as a Christmas gift to myself. It reminded me of the coat I'd had when I lived in New York and had been a successful children's clothing designer before my world had blown up. Now, living back at home in Harland Creek, I was finding my footing again and dipping my toe back into the design world while working at my mom's quilt shop.

"I'm ready, Dove. Weenie said she'll be expecting me," Mom called out from the front of the store.

The phone trilled in the darkened shop. "Let the answering machine get it," I shouted.

"Hello?" My mom's voice echoed in the empty shop.

I groaned, hoping this would not be a long, drawn-out conversation. We needed to get home soon.

I walked over to Mom, who had a puzzled look on her face. She held the phone away from her ear and blinked before hanging up.

"Who was it?" I asked, unease snaking around in my stomach.

"I don't know." The color had gone out of her face.

"Did they say anything?" I asked.

Mom looked at me and swallowed. "They said, 'She

knows too much.'" She glanced at the phone and wrung her hands together.

"Was it a man's or a woman's voice?" I prodded.

"A man's voice." Mom shook her head, went over to the cutting table, and gathered up the fabric she'd set aside for Weenie.

I shrugged. "It's probably some kids messing around. School let out before noon, so they are probably at home, bored." I glanced out the picture window. "Let's go."

Mom nodded and grabbed her purse while holding the fabric to her chest.

I opened the door and held it open while Mom walked through.

I turned the sign to "Closed" and locked the door behind us.

The snow was coming down faster than before, and we carefully made it to Mom's car. I motioned for her to get in the passenger seat. "I'll drive and just leave my car here. I've lived in New York and know how to drive in icy weather."

Mom nodded and squinted against the snowflakes pummeling her in the face as she got into the car.

Once she shut the door, I slid into the driver's seat and started the engine.

Unlike my car, Mom's Buick roared to life on the first try.

I eased my way down the street toward Mom's house.

"Wait, you're going the wrong way. We need to go by Weenie's house so I can drop this fabric off before we go home."

I shook my head. "I'm dropping you off at home first, and then I'll run over to Weenie's house. No reason for both of us to be out in this weather. Besides, I don't need you slipping on the ice and breaking a hip. Then who would run the quilt shop?" I shot her an affectionate look.

She snorted but didn't argue. "Fine. But be careful and keep your phone with you in case you have car trouble."

I nodded and kept my eyes on the street.

When I pulled up to Mom's house, I kept the car running. I went around to the passenger side of the car and helped her up the steps to the front door. I waited until she was safely inside before heading back to the car.

I pulled away from Mom's house and slowly made my way to Weenie's house.

Weenie lived a few miles outside Harland Creek in a small white house in the countryside. She was a retired librarian who had never married. I had gotten close to Weenie and the other members of the town's quilting group when I had moved back to Harland Creek.

Among the ladies, she had a quieter demeanor, and I was drawn to her kindness.

I turned onto the road leading up to Weenie's white house. I smiled when I saw her Christmas decorations still adorning the front porch. It was January, and most of the townspeople had already taken down their holiday décor.

I pulled up in front of her house and killed the engine. Reaching over to the passenger seat, I grabbed the stack of fabric.

I made my way up to the front porch and noticed the accumulation of snow on the steps. I knocked on the door and waited.

When Weenie didn't answer, I briefly wondered if she might be out. I glanced at the carport and spotted her Cadillac. Cupping my hand to my face, I peered through the glass of the door.

The house was dark.

"Weenie. It's Dove. I have your fabric," I called out and squinted through the glass.

Something felt off, and I worried maybe Weenie had fallen and hurt herself.

Cradling the fabric to my chest, I hurried around to the back of the house. When I reached the back door my heart dropped in my chest. My blood ran cold.

The back door was cracked.

Swallowing hard, I pushed the creaking door open. "Weenie. It's Dove."

I stepped inside.

Just then, Weenie popped up from behind the kitchen island. She was wide-eyed and had a knife in her hand.

"Weenie? Are you okay?"

Weenie looked at me and then down at the floor in front of her.

It was then that I noticed the feet poking out from behind the kitchen island.

I slowly walked around the island. The fabric slipped out of my hands and landed on the floor.

Lying on the floor was Louie Davis, the town's local thug. From the gray color of his face, I knew he was dead.

I looked over at Weenie, still holding the large knife in her hand.

"Weenie, what happened?" I asked as my heart thudded in my chest.

She blinked behind her large glasses like a skinny, frazzled owl. "He shouldn't have stolen my pie."

CHAPTER 2

*D*ean Gray, the town's chief of police—and my good-looking boyfriend—sat on the couch beside me and put his arm around me. "Are you okay, Dove?"

I swallowed the nausea in my throat and nodded. I pressed my hands into the couch on either side of my legs, trying to warm them up. "I'm fine. I'm more worried about Weenie. I think she was in shock when I walked in." I glanced over my shoulder into the kitchen, where the police were questioning the old woman. I looked back at Dean. "How did Louie die?"

Dean cocked his head. "There's a stab wound in his chest."

I felt a new wave of nausea. "But I didn't see any blood. If I had, I would be passed out on the floor."

It was common knowledge that I always fainted at the sight of blood.

"The stab wound wasn't very deep. I don't know if that's the actual cause of death. We won't know anything until the autopsy is complete." He eyed me. "How was Weenie acting when you walked in?"

I swallowed hard. "Dean don't jump to conclusions. Louie

was a bad guy. I don't think Weenie had anything to do with killing him."

He narrowed his eyes at me. "Dove, you said yourself that Weenie was standing over the body with a knife."

I lifted my chin. "A knife that had no blood on it."

He shrugged. "She could have wiped off the blood before you came inside."

I shook my head. "Weenie didn't kill Louie. It's impossible. But even if she did, he broke into her house, so it could have been self-defense. I mean, he was always breaking into people's homes. He wasn't exactly an upstanding guy." I bit my lip as I thought back to the strange phone call Mom had received at the quilt shop.

She knows too much.

Did that have anything to do with Louie's murder?

"So you came over to drop off some fabric and ended up coming through the back door?" Dean cocked his head.

I nodded. "Yes, the front door was locked, and I was afraid Weenie had fallen since she didn't answer the door. When I reached the back door, it was cracked open." I pressed my hand to my heart. "Dean, there was no broken glass. Weenie would not have let Louie in. How did Louie get into her house?"

Dean stood and ran his hand through his hair. "I want an officer to drive you home."

I stood and pressed my lips into a thin line. "No. I can drive myself home. Mom already heard what happened and has been blowing up my phone with questions. I told her I'm all right, but I need to get home to reassure her. You know how mothers can be."

Dean wrapped his arm around my shoulder and pulled me into a hug. I normally didn't like public signs of affection, but today I needed to feel his reassuring strength.

I melted into his protective chest, letting his warmth sink into my soul.

When I pulled back, I saw the concern in his eyes.

"What will happen to Weenie?" I asked.

Dean sighed heavily. "She needs to come to the police station and give a proper report. Because of the inclement weather, she can come in when the roads are better. It's not like she's going to skip town or anything."

I glared. "She didn't do it, Dean."

Dean cocked his head. "Look, Dove. I know you want to help your friend, but please, for the love of God, stay out of this investigation. And keep the quilting ladies out of it as well." He squeezed my hand one last time before heading to the kitchen.

There was a loud commotion and shouting coming from the front porch before the front door flew open.

"Where is she?" Bertha Mills stormed into the house, elbowing two large police officers out of her way. Bertha was one of the quilting ladies and had quite the reputation of getting her way. Where Weenie was quiet and kind, Bertha was loud and obnoxious.

"Bertha?" I blinked. "What are you doing here?"

Bertha shot me a glare. "I'm here to stay with Weenie. I heard what happened to Louie and how the police are trying to pin his murder on an old woman."

Weenie slid out of the chair at the kitchen island and lifted her slender chin. "I'm not that old, Bertha. You're older than me."

Bertha looked at her friend and held up her hand. "Don't say another word, Weenie. Not until you speak to your lawyer."

Weenie shoved her large glasses up on the bridge of her nose and squinted. "But I don't have a lawyer."

Bertha smirked. "You do now. Alfred, get your skinny

butt in here," Bertha bellowed.

A fragile-looking old man carrying a briefcase shuffled into the house. He smiled and held out a business card.

Bertha snorted, grabbed the card, and shoved it into Dean's face. "Look here, Mr. Fancy Pants. Weenie now has legal representation. This is Alfred Heffner, attorney at law. I've watched enough police movies to know you can't ask her questions without her lawyer present."

Weenie opened her mouth, but Bertha wagged a finger in her direction. "Not a word, Weenie."

Weenie slammed her mouth shut and looked a bit put out.

I looked at Weenie. "Weenie, I don't think you should stay here tonight."

Dean nodded. "Dove's right. The police will pull an all-night investigation at the crime scene. Would you mind taking her to your mom's house, Dove?"

I smiled at the old woman. "Not at all. Weenie, why don't I get you some clothes and some overnight items?"

Weenie frowned and wrung her hands. "I hate to be a bother."

I shook my head. "It's no bother at all. I'll be right back." I headed down the hall toward Weenie's bedroom. Sloan Jackson, one of Harland Creek's police officers, was going through Weenie's drawers, looking for evidence. He looked up when I entered.

"I'm taking Weenie home with me. I need a change of clothes for her. Mind if I gather some items?"

Sloan shook his head and closed the drawer. "Go right ahead. There is nothing in here of any interest. I think I'm done looking." Sloan started for the door but then stopped and looked at me. "Dove?"

I pulled a small overnight bag out of Weenie's closet and looked at Sloan. "Yes?"

Sloan narrowed his eyes on me. "If you find something, let us know." He turned and walked out of the room.

I rolled my eyes.

It was no secret I, and my group of quilting ladies, had a knack for solving crime. Often, it rubbed the police department the wrong way when we were right. And lately, we had been consistently right.

I brushed off Sloan's comment, went to Weenie's dresser, and opened the top drawer. After gathering some underwear, socks, pajamas, toothbrush, and a couple of changes of clothes, I zipped the bag and headed back to the kitchen.

The police had congregated in the kitchen where the body had been. Thankfully, the coroner had removed it, so I didn't have to look at Louie's colorless face anymore.

Louie had moved to our small town from Brooklyn, New York, a few years back.

He had been Gertrude Brown's hired muscle who collected rent from her tenants in the long term RV/trailer park she owned, the Chateau RV Park. Louie also had a practice of breaking into people's homes and stealing from them. People feared Louie and his threats, so no one ever pressed charges. After Gertrude's death, Louie had inherited everything from her.

Weenie had confided in me that she found Louie in her home a few years ago, standing in her kitchen and eating her pie. She didn't report him because she feared the repercussions.

Once Dean had become chief of police, Louie had stopped breaking into people's homes.

It was ironic to me that Louie had met his death in Weenie's house, of all places. Weenie was petite and scrawny and couldn't hurt a fly.

Shaking off my morbid thoughts, I walked over to Weenie, who was standing by the window and staring out at the front yard as the snow came down. Bertha had left with the lawyer.

"Weenie, I've got some clothes packed for you. Is there anything else you want to bring?"

Weenie turned her gray head toward me. "I'd like to take my knitting." She pointed toward a basket by her recliner. "It's over there."

I smiled. "I'll get it for you." I walked over and packed up her knitting into the weekender bag. "Ready?"

She looked so sad and small standing in the living room. She nodded once and walked to the front door, where I met her.

I opened the door and held her hand as we walked down the icy steps together. I opened the passenger-side door and assisted her inside before putting her bag in the backseat.

Sliding into the driver's seat, I started the engine and carefully drove down the driveway.

The weather man on the radio was giving an update on Mississippi's crazy winter weather.

I tried starting a conversation, but it was obvious Weenie was in no mood to talk.

When I pulled up to Mom's house, the front door swung open, and Mom stepped out onto the front porch with a quilt wrapped around her shoulders. She gave a quick wave and motioned for us to hurry up and come inside.

I killed the engine and made my way over to the other side of the car.

I grabbed Weenie's bag before opening her door to help her out.

Weenie eased out of the car, and I shut the door behind her.

"Come on inside. I made some potato soup. It will warm you up," Mom called out.

"I hope you're hungry, Weenie. Mom's potato soup is the best," I said softly.

Weenie said nothing but took an awkward step on an icy patch. She stumbled, and I reached out and grabbed her arm and righted her.

"Are you okay?"

Weenie winced and pulled her arm out of my reach. She cradled her arm to her chest.

I helped her up to the front porch and into the warmth of the house.

"Let me see your arm." I helped her get her coat off and shoved up the sleeve of her gray sweatsuit.

I gasped at the bruises on her arm. They were in the shape of large fingerprints.

"Weenie, did Louie hurt you?" I asked softly.

Weenie looked at me behind her large glasses and blinked. "I told him he should have left my pie alone."

CHAPTER 3

*W*e had eaten dinner and gotten Weenie settled into the guest room before I filled Mom in on everything that had happened.

"Do you think Weenie killed Louie?" Mom looked at me with worry in her eyes.

I shook my head. "I don't see how. She is so much smaller than Louie. There is no way she could have overpowered him."

Mom worried her hands together. "But you said she was standing over him with a knife in her hand. Not to mention the bruises on her arm. She said herself that he should not have touched her pie."

I cringed. "I know it sounds bad, but she never admitted to killing him. Besides, there was no blood. I can't believe that Weenie could have killed him. Not Weenie." Weenie's words about how Louie shouldn't have touched her pie kept playing in my mind.

Mom's phone rang, and I jumped. She reached out and answered it.

When Mom ended the call, she looked up at me. "That

was Bertha. She wants a meeting for us to get a list of suspects together."

I sighed and rested my head back against the couch. "Mom, I think that's a bad idea. You know the police don't like us interfering." I cut my eyes at her.

She didn't have to say a word. From the look she was shooting me, I knew there was no use in arguing.

I stood. "Fine. But there's no way we can meet tonight because of the weather. I'll get the whiteboard ready to take notes."

Mom nodded slowly. "I bought a new one and put it in the closet. That way, we have a whiteboard here and one at the quilt shop. We have our first suspect, so we might as well put her name up. We just need to know what to call her."

I shook my head. "This whole thing is crazy."

Mom brightened slightly. "Yes, it is. And that's what we can call Weenie. Crazy Quilt."

I grimaced. "That's kind of cruel, don't you think?"

Mom shot me a withering look. "I'm not calling Weenie crazy. I'm saying this whole thing is crazy. I'm surprised at you, Dove. How could you think I would call Weenie crazy?"

My shoulders slumped, and I rubbed my eyes. "I'm sorry. This whole day has me rattled."

Mom stood from her chair, walked over to me and sat down beside me. She reached for my hand and squeezed it. "I'm sorry too. It's been a long day for everyone."

I nodded. "True."

The lights flickered and then went out.

"I'll get a flashlight. Don't move." I stood and carefully felt my way to the kitchen. I opened the junk drawer and pawed around until I found the flashlight. I clicked it on and walked back into the living room.

"The heat is off. We might as well go to bed and snuggle

under some quilts. We will figure things out regarding Weenie in the morning," I stated.

Mom didn't argue but walked upstairs with me. I shone the light in her room and helped her find the flashlight in her nightstand. She grabbed some quilts out of the closet and put them on top of her bed to keep her warm.

Mom grabbed a colorful Sunbonnet Sue quilt and a red-and-yellow Log Cabin quilt from her closet. "Dove, put these on top of Weenie. She's as skinny as a rail. She needs these to stay warm tonight."

I said goodnight and headed to the guest room. I eased the door open and found Weenie fast asleep. I laid the flashlight on the dresser and gently layered the quilts on top of her. Glancing around the room, I found a crocheted blanket that Mom had made years ago and added it on top of Weenie as well before sneaking out of the room.

Shutting the door to my room, I walked over to the window and looked out. The streetlights were out, but I could hear the wind howling through the tree-lined street. The snow had turned to ice, and pellets were bouncing off my window.

Shivering, I stepped away from the window and quickly found my flannel pajamas and slipped them on.

Walking to my closet, I found two quilts, a Jacob's Ladder and a Grandmother's Flower Garden, and put them on top of my comforter. I laid my flashlight on the nightstand before slipping under the heavy weight of the quilts.

Silence filled the room as the elements outside beat against the house while I was snug in my cocoon.

CHAPTER 4

"*T*he roads are too bad to travel, so we are just going to stay put," I stated as I stared outside. There was a thick layer of ice along the power lines. We still didn't have power. I'd gotten up early to start a fire in the fireplace and boiled some water on the gas stove so I could make coffee. I figured it would keep us warm while we waited for the electricity to come back on.

"But I need to get home." Weenie frowned.

I pressed a cup of hot coffee into her bony hands and tried to reassure her. "I know, Weenie, but no one is traveling right now. Dean called this morning and said the power company is trying its best to get the power back on as soon as possible. Your house is outside the city limits, and it's going to be one of the last homes to get electricity. It's safer if you just stay with us for now."

"I hate to be so much trouble." Weenie tasted her coffee and gave me and Mom a worried look.

"You are never any trouble, Weenie. We love having you," Mom insisted. Just then, her cell phone rang. She reached for it to answer. "Hello?"

I watched her face as her lips pressed together in a thin line. She glanced over at Weenie and then looked away.

I tried to make out who was on the other end of the line but couldn't.

Mom ended the call and looked at me.

"Who was that?" I asked.

She took a sip of her coffee. "That was one of the police officers. Some new guy. He was telling me that I need to bring Weenie to the police station to make a proper report."

I cringed. "In road conditions like this? Is he crazy?"

Mom snorted. "He sounded like he was from New York. I heard Dean say he was hiring a new guy. Apparently, he is used to traveling on icy roads."

I looked over at Weenie.

She gripped her coffee cup with both hands. I noticed her wrinkled hands tremble slightly.

"Weenie, are you okay?"

She glanced over at me. "I'm guessing the whole town thinks I'm a murderer, don't they, Dove?"

My eyes widened slightly. I set my cup down and stood. Walking over to Weenie's chair, I knelt beside her. "Everyone knows you couldn't hurt a fly." I squeezed her arm.

She gave me a tired smile. "You know how people are. They love juicy gossip."

I bit my lip.

Weenie was right. Harland Creek would obviously know what happened yesterday. Everyone would have heard the news by now.

The phone rang again, and I jumped.

Mom reached for it and answered. "Hello?"

I stood and walked back to my seat. I sat and reached for my coffee.

Mom said a few words before she hung up. Her face went pale.

"That was Elizabeth Harland. She said Petunia went missing last night."

CHAPTER 5

We were all huddled around the fireplace when I heard a knock at the door.

I tossed off the throw, stood, and headed to the front door.

I threw open the door and saw Dean standing there.

Despite the dark circles under his eyes from working all night, he gave me a smile. "Dove."

I pulled him inside out of the cold and wrapped my arms around his chilly neck. Every time I hugged Dean, the world seemed to melt away.

When I pulled back, I looked into his eyes. "Long night?"

He ran his hand across his face. "Yeah. I'm here to take Weenie to the station to make a statement."

I nodded. "Want some coffee?" I headed toward the kitchen without waiting for an answer.

"I would love some." His boots fell heavily on the floor behind me as he followed me into the kitchen.

I reached for the coffeepot and poured Dean a cup of black coffee.

He took it and lifted it to his lips. He smiled. "That's good.

Much better than the coffee at the police station." He eased down into a kitchen chair.

I sat beside him. "Any news on the murder?"

Dean took another sip and shook his head. "No. I'm hoping Weenie can shed some light on some things." He glanced to the living room. "Is she up?"

I nodded. "Yes, she's been up since early this morning. We've been drinking coffee around the fireplace since we can't watch the news." I frowned. "Any idea how long the electricity will be off?"

Dean sat back in his chair. "They had linemen working all night across the state. Half the state is without electricity. Hopefully they can get electricity restored in Harland Creek soon, but they are concentrating on the larger cities first."

I crossed my arms. That meant I was going to have to wait on a hot bath.

Dean stood. "I need to get Weenie down to the station. The weather has really put us behind on this case."

I grabbed his empty cup and placed it beside mine in the sink. "Is her attorney going to be present?" I turned and looked at him.

He pulled a face. "Alfred Heffner? I can't imagine what Bertha thought she was doing dragging that man to Weenie's house last night. He's a horrible attorney. I wouldn't pay him to represent Tarzan."

I bit back a grin at the mention of Tarzan, Dean's German shepherd, who was also the K9 for the police department.

He shot me a look and lowered his voice. "I'm serious, Dove. Alfred has no business still practicing law."

My smile slipped. "Maybe I should go with Weenie. She shouldn't be by herself."

He studied me for a second. "Fine. You can come, but don't interfere with the investigation."

I brightened. "I won't."

I followed him into the living room, where Weenie and Mom were sitting covered up with quilts.

"Dean. How are the roads?" Mom looked at him.

He snorted. "Not good. I'm in my four-wheel-drive truck with snow tires. We put snow tires on the police vehicles when we heard the snow was coming." He glanced over at Weenie and smiled. "Hi, Weenie."

Her gray head poked out from the thick layer of quilts wrapped around her. She blinked behind her thick glasses, looking very much like a frazzled owl.

"Hello, Dean." Weenie's voice was small as she looked at him. "Are you here to arrest me?"

Dean looked startled. "I'm only here to take you down to the station so you can give a statement of what happened."

Weenie blinked again. "I guess I need to get my shoes on."

I looked from Weenie to Dean. "And I'm coming with you."

Weenie slowly uncovered the quilts from around her body and stood. She made her way over to the front door, where she found her shoes from the night before.

I quickly slipped on my shoes and grabbed our coats. I helped Weenie into hers and then slipped mine on. I thought about the marks on Weenie's arm, but I didn't want to bring them up to Dean. It wasn't because I thought she was guilty —I didn't. I just didn't want to give him any evidence that might make her look bad.

"Hold on to Dean walking down the steps, Weenie. Everything is slick," I stated.

"I've got you, Weenie." Dean wrapped a protective arm around the old woman as they walked outside.

I held on to the outdoor furniture as I made my way across the porch and down toward Dean's police truck.

My breath was visible as I snuggled down in my coat and wrapped my scarf tighter against my neck. The snow had stopped, but the icy wind was still whipping through the lacy trees lining our street. The sky was overcast with dark, gray, menacing clouds.

Dean opened the passenger door and assisted Weenie inside the truck. I opened the back door, hoisted myself into the seat, and quickly shut the door against the wind.

We watched as Dean walked around the front of the truck to the driver's side and climbed in.

"I guess you heard about Petunia," I said. "Has she been found?"

Dean started the engine and shook his head. "Not yet. Sloan told me that Grayson was trying to get a group of people together to go look for her last night, but the weather was so bad."

My heart tugged in my chest. "Heather must be so worried."

Weenie looked back at me. "After we leave the police station, we should go over to Elizabeth's and see what we can do. I know she's heartbroken and worried sick. She loved that little goat like a granddaughter."

I nodded.

Dean pulled onto the street and shook his head. "You shouldn't be driving with road conditions like this, Dove. It's too dangerous. Wait until the streets melt some."

Weenie shook her head but said nothing.

For the rest of the drive to the police station, everyone was silent as we watched the winter scene outside our windows.

When Dean pulled into the parking spot and got out, we stayed seated.

Weenie turned in her seat. "Don't worry, Dove. We'll help look for Petunia after this."

CHAPTER 6

I looked around the police station from Dean's office. Weenie sat quietly next to me with her hands clasped together in her lap.

The scent of coffee mingled with the odor of disinfectant from someone mopping up the wet footprints at the front door hung heavy in the air.

Dean walked in and placed two cups of coffee in front of us.

Weenie winced and held her bony hands up. "No thank you, Dean. I've had enough coffee for one day. One more cup and I'll jump out of my skin."

He gave her an understanding smile. "That's okay, Weenie." He set the extra cup down on his desk and eased down into his seat. "Now, do you have any questions before we get started?"

She leaned forward a little. "Have you had any word on Petunia? I didn't know if someone called in a lead since we've been here. You could send a patrol car out to look for her."

Dean blinked and slowly shook his head. "I've been kind

of busy working on this murder case, Weenie. This takes precedence over a missing goat."

Weenie gave an uncharacteristic angry little snort. "I wouldn't give two cents worrying about who did Louie in. No one liked him, anyway."

Dean narrowed his eyes slightly. "Weenie, can you tell me how Louie came to be in your house?"

Weenie sat back in her chair. "I was in my sewing room when I heard a noise. It was snowing hard, so I thought maybe it was my pipes creaking or something. When I walked out into the kitchen, I saw Louie lying on the floor, not moving."

Dean looked over at me and then back at Weenie. "And Dove came in and said she found you standing over the body, holding a knife."

Weenie blinked. "If that's what she said, then that's what happened."

Dean blew out a breath. "Weenie, why did you have a knife in your hand?"

I shifted in my seat. As much as I didn't like Alfred, I also didn't want Weenie to say something she would later regret. "Dean, shouldn't Weenie have her attorney present?" I looked over at her. "Weenie, do you want me to call him?"

Weenie looked at me through her glasses. "Do you think I should, Dove?"

I bit my lip. I could tell Dean was getting agitated with my interference. But I didn't care. Weenie was old and forgetful. She might accidentally say the wrong thing and incriminate herself.

"I think it would be best," I stated.

Dean stood. "Fine. You can use my phone to call him." He pointed to the landline on his desk before he left the office.

Weenie pulled a card out of her black purse and held it out to me. "Dove, do you mind calling?"

I smiled and took the card. "Sure." I quickly dialed the number and spoke to Mr. Heffner while I eyed Weenie.

I ended the call and looked at my friend. "Weenie, Mr. Heffner seems to be iced in at his house. He said not to say anything more until he is with you. They can't keep you here if your attorney isn't here to represent you while you are being questioned."

Weenie nodded slowly.

I glanced at the door to make sure no one was nearby. "Weenie, do you mind telling me what you were doing with a knife in your hand?"

Weenie shrugged. "I heard a noise, so I took the knife out of my sewing cabinet to go check it out."

I frowned. "So, you didn't really think it was the pipes you heard?"

She frowned and looked straight ahead. "It's not safe for a woman to live alone, Dove. Louie has broken into my house before."

I nodded. "I remember you telling me that. You said he stole a pie."

Weenie lifted her chin. "Sure did. And he stood in my kitchen smirking as he ate the whole thing. He said if I told the police, he would come back and hurt me. So, I kept my mouth shut."

I cocked my head. "Weenie, how did Louie get into your house the first time?"

She sighed. "He picked the lock. After that, I had more modern locks put on, and he never came back." She glanced out the window. "But I think the reason he didn't come back was that Dean had gotten the position of chief of police. And I think Louie knew Dean wasn't scared of him."

I nodded. "I think you're right. Do you know how he got in this time?"

She shrugged. "I don't know. I didn't have time to look around. Then you walked in the back door."

I frowned. "The back door was ajar when I came in. Maybe Louie picked the lock."

Weenie frowned and shook her head. "That's impossible. The back door has a coded lock. You must punch in the right code before it opens. There's no way he would know the code."

I tried to rack my brain but couldn't come up how Louie had unlocked the door.

Dean stepped into the office. "Is your attorney coming?"

Weenie shook her head. "He's iced in. He said you can't question me without his presence."

Dean nodded. "That is correct. I'll take you back to Mildred's house…"

Weenie frowned. "Can't I go back to my own house?"

Dean glanced over at me for help. "I wasn't sure if you wanted to go back there just yet. It's isolated and far from town. Besides, Dove will probably get electricity before you do. It's probably best to go back to her house."

I nodded. "Yes, Weenie. I know you want to get back to your house, but we'd love to have you stay with us."

Weenie worried her hands together. "I don't know."

There was a loud commotion outside the office, and Dean's door suddenly flew open. Standing there in large boots and an ugly brown overcoat was Bertha.

"Dean, you know you can't question the suspect without her attorney," Bertha boomed.

Weenie's eyes widened. "Dean, you think I'm a suspect?"

Dean stood and glared at Bertha. "You're not supposed to just barge in here like this."

Bertha parked her hands on her hips and shot daggers at him. "Who's going to stop me?"

Sloan walked past the office door and shook his head, agreeing with her logic.

"I'm not questioning her, Bertha. I was about to take her and Dove home. "

Bertha held out her hand. "There is no need. I'll do it."

Weenie grimaced. "Can you drive on these roads, Bertha?"

Bertha lifted her chin. "Of course I can. I've driven my van during a blizzard in Montana. Only slid off the road once."

I pulled a face. That did not make me feel any better.

"Fine. Take them home but be careful." Dean stood and walked out of the office.

I stood with my hands clenched at my side. I could not believe Dean was going to let me get in a vehicle with Bertha. I really thought he cared more about me than that.

I looked over at Weenie. "Come on, Weenie. Let's go home. "

CHAPTER 7

"*B*ertha, I think you need to slow down a bit." I tightened my grip on the door handle of the van.

"I'm an expert at driving in the snow, Dove. I can drive in any conditions, rain or snow." Bertha lifted her chin and sped up a bit.

"You should work for the post office, Bertha. They can always use dependable workers. They don't seem to be doing a very good job. My mail certainly has been getting lost lately," Weenie said from her position perched on a folding chair. Weenie's chair skidded an inch to the left when Bertha swerved to miss a squirrel who darted out in the middle of the road.

Bertha's van was an oddity. She had taken the back seats out to make more room. If she ever had to drive more than one person around, she would just stick a plastic folding chair in the back. She didn't even try to secure it to the floor.

"I'm pretty sure your setup is illegal, Bertha. If Dean saw that, he'd give you a ticket." I pointed to the plastic chair.

Bertha glared at me. "You better not rat me out to your boyfriend, Dove."

My eyes widened at the signal light ahead that had turned red. "Bertha, look!"

Bertha applied the brakes a little too hard, and Weenie's chair, went sliding up between our seats. I threw my arm out and stopped her from going any farther.

Weenie looked over at me and smiled. "Thanks, Dove."

My heart was in my chest. "Bertha…"

An older-model Buick passed in front of us, and I did a double-take. "Hey, did you see who that was?"

Bertha shot another dagger at me. "No, I was too busy being yelled at."

I motioned for her to follow the car. "That. Right there. That was Polly O'Hara."

Bertha gave me an odd look. "The romance author?"

Weenie's eyes widened. "Didn't she have a romantic relationship with Louie?"

A slow smile crossed my face. "She sure did. And she hasn't been in Harland Creek in months."

Bertha cocked her head. "Odd that she shows up and Louie is found dead."

I nodded. "That's exactly what I was thinking. Bertha, follow her."

Bertha did as I asked and followed Polly toward the Chateau RV Park. Polly was obviously used to driving on iced roads because she didn't slow down one bit.

Polly finally pulled into the aging RV park and promptly parked behind an older-model RV before carefully climbing out of the car.

"Wait, that's not the same RV Polly used to have. This one is smaller and older. In fact, it looks like it's barely holding together." My gaze roamed over the dated RV, which had plastic taped over the windows. Polly walked over to the door of the RV and stuck her key in. She wiggled it, but the door didn't give. Finally, after a few curse words and some tugging, the door came free.

Stomping her feet on the steps to knock off the snow, she then stepped inside and slammed the door behind her.

"She's going to freeze to death in that tin can," Bertha said dryly.

"I guess the RV park doesn't have any electricity, either." I looked around and saw a few of the patrons of the park bundled up in heavy coats and huddled together over firepits to warm themselves.

I pulled out my phone.

"What are you doing, Dove?" Weenie asked.

"I'm sending a text to Dean. He needs to know that Polly is back in town." I gave Bertha a knowing look.

"Which means the suspect pool in Louie's death just grew a little bit bigger," Bertha said.

Weenie frowned. "Why would she kill Louie? I thought she loved him."

Bertha snorted. "There's a fine line between love and hate."

I contemplated Bertha's words.

"I find it suspicious that Polly shows up in Harland Creek when her 'boyfriend' is murdered. Maybe they broke up a while ago, maybe not. But I think this is something that needs to be investigated further." I sent a quick text to Dean and waited for his reply.

He told me he would send someone over to question Polly.

I looked at Bertha. "Can you run me by the shop so I can drive my car home?"

I didn't want to be without my car. Who knew where I'd have to travel to get this case solved and Weenie out of trouble.

CHAPTER 8

*B*y the time Bertha pulled up to Mom's house, there was another car in the driveway. I immediately recognized it as Elizabeth Harland's vehicle.

We carefully got out of Bertha's van and slowly made our way into the house.

The warmth of the fireplace pulled us into the living room.

"Elizabeth, Agnes, did you find Petunia?" I asked as I pulled my coat off.

Elizabeth's brow furrowed, and she clasped the coffee mug between her hands. She was sitting on the couch beside Agnes, who had her arm around her friend.

"No, I haven't. Heather and Grayson got up early this morning and started looking again. But with this new blanket of snow on the ground, it makes it hard to find any tracks." She looked so worried over the little goat.

Agnes shook her head. "This isn't like Petunia. She is always such a good girl. She would never just wander off. I wonder if someone stole her."

Elizabeth sucked in a gasp at the notion. "Kidnapped?"

I shook my head. "Don't jump to conclusions. We don't know if that's the case." I sat down in the chair next to Elizabeth. "When was the last time you saw Petunia?"

Elizabeth took a deep breath and blew it out. "Well, Heather was going to bring her inside when the weather started getting bad. We saw Petunia playing by the barn that afternoon." Elizabeth smiled. "Heather bought an old slide at a yard sale and put it beside the barn for Petunia to play. She loves jumping off it."

Agnes frowned. "Does she slide down it at all?"

Elizabeth's eyebrows went up slightly. "Only if Heather is sliding down and holding her in her lap."

I blinked, trying to imagine the scene. I then shook my head. "Okay, so you saw her by the barn?"

Elizabeth nodded. "Yes. She never wanders off, and we had gotten busy covering some of the more delicate bulbs in the field. Anyway, when it started snowing, we went inside, and that's when we realized we forgot to bring Petunia in. "

Agnes nodded. "Which is odd because it's hard to forget her. When she's playing, she always bleats."

Elizabeth set her cup down and wrung her hands together. "Heather went outside. After a while, when she didn't come in, I went out to check on them. Heather came running to the house saying she couldn't find Petunia anywhere." Elizabeth's shoulders slumped. "We called Grayson, and he came over. He and Heather looked for Petunia until the roads weren't safe to travel."

My heart tightened in my chest. I was beginning to get worried about the little goat.

She was my crime-solving partner, and we had grown close. I didn't want anything to happen to her.

"Grayson and Heather have been out looking for her since dawn. They called the police station to get some help, but they are busy..." Elizabeth's voice trailed off as she glanced over at Weenie.

"They're busy investigating Louie's murder." Weenie blinked. "I don't know why they are wasting time on that guy. No one liked him." She glanced around the room.

Bertha narrowed her eyes on her friend. "Weenie, how did Louie end up in your home?"

Weenie shrugged her slight shoulders. "I guess he just walked in. I was sewing and heard something in the kitchen. So, I grabbed my knife and found him on the floor."

I blinked. "And then I showed up."

Weenie looked over at me. "I'm still not sure how he got in. I had new keyless locks put on my doors, and I am positive he didn't know the combination."

Bertha clapped her hands together once. "I know there is a lot going on right now with Petunia, but we also need to think about Weenie. Right now, the police are looking at her hard since the body was found in her house. We need to put our heads together and look at other potential suspects."

Agnes nodded. "Bertha is right." She cut her eyes at Bertha. "And that's not something you'll hear me say every day."

Bertha growled.

I stood and walked over to the whiteboard I had shoved in the corner of the room. "I think that's a good idea." I grabbed the dry-erase marker.

"Crazy Quilt." Weenie read the words on the board. "Is that me?"

I held my breath. I didn't want to hurt her feelings.

Mom smiled. "I told Dove you were working on a crazy quilt. I thought it might be a good name."

Weenie smiled. "I love making crazy quilts. You don't have to follow directions and it still comes out pretty."

I smiled. "I like them too, Weenie."

Bertha cleared her throat. "We need to add another suspect to the list."

Mom's eyebrows shot up. "The police have another suspect?"

Bertha shook her head. "Not exactly. But on our way over here, guess who we spotted in town?"

When no one answered, Bertha poked out her chest. "Polly O'Hara."

Elizabeth gasped. "The romance author?"

I nodded. "Yes, and we followed her back to where she is staying at the Chateau RV Park. It seems she has traded her fancy RV in for something more…" I was searching for the right word.

"Something old and run-down." Weenie offered.

Mom frowned. "So, her finances are strained?"

I shrugged. "It looks that way. But I want to know why she is back in Harland Creek."

Agnes cocked her head. "Maybe she came back to Harland Creek to see Louie and ask for some money. Didn't they have a romantic relationship the last time she was here?"

I nodded. "Yes. And it's very suspicious that when she comes to town, Louie ends up dead."

Bertha cleared her throat. "Maybe she killed him when he refused to give her any money."

I frowned. "But why wouldn't he give her money? I mean, clearly, he cared for her."

Bertha snorted. "Men are fickle like that. One minute they are spouting poetry and giving you flowers, the next they are cold as ice."

Agnes narrowed her eyes on Bertha. "Is that what happened to your last husband, Bertha? He did you wrong, and you slipped him something in your pound cake?"

Bertha shot daggers at Agnes.

Agnes shrugged. "I'm just asking. I wouldn't blame you if you did." She turned her attention back to the whiteboard. "So what name are we going to call Polly?"

I frowned. "What name did we give her last time?"

Mom stood and walked over to the decorative table in the corner. "Let me see. I wrote it down." She pulled out a notebook from a drawer and flipped through the pages.

She ran her finger down a page and smiled. "Here it is. House That Jack Built."

Agnes nodded. "I remember now. We named her that quilt block because she lost the house in her divorce and ended up in the fancy RV. Dove write her name down on the board."

I quickly jotted down the quilt block, House That Jack Built, and looked back at the ladies. "In order for Polly to be a strong suspect, we need to find out where she was when Louie was killed."

Elizabeth frowned "Speaking of... do we have cause of death yet? I find it very odd that the man shows up at Weenie's kitchen and dies on her floor. His truck wasn't outside her house, so how did he get there?"

I nodded and tapped the dry-erase marker against my lip. "Those are very good questions that we need to find the answers to."

CHAPTER 9

I grabbed my ringing phone off the coffee table. I
excused myself from the ladies and headed into
the kitchen.

"Dean, what's up?" I kept my voice down so the ladies
couldn't hear my conversation.

"We got an official cause of death."

My eyes grew wide. "What is it?"

There was a silence before he spoke.

"Louie was poisoned."

I gasped. "What? Poisoned? What kind of poison?"

He cleared his throat. "Yes, poisoned. And I can't tell you
with what."

"What about the stab wound?" I asked.

"The coroner said it wasn't a fatal wound and didn't hit
any major vessels. That's why there wasn't much blood. He
was already dead when he was stabbed."

My stomach rolled at the mention of blood. I swallowed
hard and cleared my throat.

"Look, Dove. I'm already telling you too much as it is. The

question is, was he poisoned in Weenie's house? Or was he poisoned before he stepped foot inside?"

I narrowed my eyes and wished he could see the look I was giving him. "Dean, you know that Weenie didn't poison Louie. The real suspect is still out there." I licked my lips. "You know Polly O'Hara is staying at the Chateau RV Park, and you really need to investigate her. The fact that she had a romantic relationship with Louie puts her as a prime suspect."

He sighed loudly. "Dove, just because she had a relationship with Louie doesn't mean she killed him."

I cocked my head. "Are you telling me you don't find it suspicious that she showed up in town before Louie gets killed? I've seen documentaries that the person romantically connected with the victim is usually a suspect."

Dean grunted his frustration. "I'll check her out. In the meantime, if Elizabeth is over there, let her know someone spotted Petunia behind the grocery store."

The weight lifted off my shoulders. "Did they catch her?" I walked back into the living room and looked at Elizabeth.

"No. It seems like Petunia wasn't alone. They reported seeing her with a couple of dogs, rummaging through a dumpster."

I smiled. "Well, at least they've seen her. I'll let Elizabeth know." I ended the call, walked into the living room, and gave Elizabeth a smile. "That was Dean. Petunia has been spotted behind the grocery store."

Elizabeth jumped up from her seat. "Thank God. I should head over to the grocery store before she runs off."

My smile slipped. "I'm sorry, Elizabeth. She's not there anymore. She ran off when someone approached her."

I watched as her joy turned to despair. I looked to Agnes for some support.

"This is a good sign, Elizabeth. You should call Heather so

she and Grayson can head over there and pick up her trail. Surely, she can't have gotten far," Agnes said enthusiastically.

Elizabeth nodded. "You're right." She reached for her purse and pulled out her phone. After a quick call to Heather, she hung up and looked around the room. "Well, what's everyone waiting for? Let's go see if we can get Petunia."

CHAPTER 10

$\mathcal{W}$e spent half an hour behind the grocery store, calling Petunia to come out of the small patch of woods behind the store.

No one knew if the little goat was still in the woods, but Elizabeth said she couldn't give up.

When Heather and Grayson pulled up beside us in his truck, we waited a little while longer while he explored the woods.

When he came out, he said Petunia was gone. They followed her tracks until the trail went cold.

I convinced the ladies to go on to Mom's quilt shop so we could get some hot coffee and warm up. Thankfully, the store had electricity back, so we could make some coffee and talk. They were all milling around the room where Mom taught quilt class while I got busy making the coffee.

"Dove," Agnes poked her head in the entrance of the kitchenette. "Where do you keep the Band-Aids?"

I turned and frowned. "Under the sink in the bathroom. Who needs a Band-Aid?"

Agnes shook her head. "Weenie. She poked her finger

with a needle, and it won't stop bleeding." She smiled. "I'll get her taken care of."

I turned my attention back to the coffeepot and filling the assorted mugs that we kept in the cabinet. None of them matched, and all of them had some form of advertising on the front.

I filled the mugs, found a tray, and carried it to the ladies.

Bertha sighed. "Finally. It took you long enough." She grabbed a cup of coffee and took a sip.

I shot her a glare, but she didn't notice.

"Don't mind her, Dove. Bertha is just irritable because she's out of fiber." Agnes deadpanned.

Bertha's face went red, and she stammered but couldn't get coherent words out.

I bit back a grin as I passed the coffee mugs to the ladies.

The bell above the front door tinkled, and I frowned. "I forgot to lock the door. But everyone should know we are closed due to the weather. I'll go see who it is."

I walked out of the room and almost ran into Maggie.

"Maggie, what are you doing here?"

She pressed her hand to her chest. "I saw the cars parked out front and decided to stop by and see if there was any word on Petunia."

I waved her toward the room where everyone was sitting.

"Maggie, what brings you here?" My mom looked at her friend. "Come on in and get some coffee." She pressed a cup of hot coffee into Maggie's hands.

"Thanks, Mildred." Maggie took a sip. "As soon as the electricity came back on, I had a flood of calls from half the women in Harland Creek, wanting their hair done." She rolled her eyes. "Sylvia and I came in and started working on them as they made their way into town. Although we had Maude and Hildie cancel because their car slid off the road."

I cringed. "I'm surprised so many women are attempting to drive with the roads like they are."

Maggie snorted. "Honey, nothing will come between a woman and a blowout." She looked around the room, and her eyes landed on Weenie. She walked over and squeezed her shoulder. "How are you holding up, Weenie? I tried calling your house last night to check on you, but no one answered."

Weenie smiled. "I spent the night at Mildred and Dove's."

Maggie nodded. "That was a good idea. You didn't need to spend the night alone. Not in that house." She looked over at me. "I'm guessing you have a suspect list ready."

I nodded. "Yes. We are working on it."

Maggie narrowed her eyes at me. "I guess you know Polly O'Hara is back in town."

I cocked my head. "How did you know this?

She smirked. "She had a hair appointment a couple of days ago."

I studied her. "Did she volunteer any information? Like how long she was going to stay in town or why she was back?"

Weenie leaned forward. "Or how her book is coming? I've been waiting for news about her new release but haven't seen anything."

Maggie shook her head. "No. She was secretive. In fact, she put her earbuds in while I did her hair. Said she was trying to concentrate to come up with the next scene in her book." Maggie narrowed her eyes. "But I think she just didn't want to talk." She snorted. "Imagine that. Coming to a hair salon and not wanting to talk."

Agnes stood and paced. "I don't know what that woman ever saw in Louie."

Maggie took a seat on the couch. "She was probably lonely. It's amazing what you put up with when you are lonely." She glanced at the whiteboard. "I think you should add another name to that board, Dove."

I blinked. "Who?"

A smirk crossed Maggie's lips. "Linda Martinez."

Elizabeth's eyes widened, and she leaned forward in her seat. "Linda lives in the RV park. Why would you think she would be a suspect?"

Maggie crossed her arms over her chest and lifted her chin. "Because she was in my chair a few days ago to get highlights." Maggie rolled her eyes. "Highlights are a bad look on her, and I've tried telling her that. The woman won't listen. She is bound and determined to look like the Harlot of Babylon."

I snickered and then bit my lip.

"Anyway, while I was doing Linda's hair, I saw a bump on the back of her head. She said Louie hit her."

The room went silent. And then Weenie spoke.

"Did she call the police on him?"

Maggie snorted. "No. She said she didn't want to get the police involved. I think because of that time she gave a bad check at the grocery store. Anyhow, they were in an argument about Louie raising the rent on her trailer. She said he was crazy and that she wasn't going to give him another cent until he fixed the plumbing issue. He said he wasn't going to sink a dime in her trailer and if she didn't pay up, he was going to evict her. She hit him on the head with a bucket full of dead squirrels."

I blinked. "Excuse me. Did you say a bucket of dead squirrels?"

Maggie nodded. "Linda hunts squirrels. And she forages for food. Says it helps her save on her grocery bill. She works part time for Farmer Brown in the spring, but during winter, work is scarce. Anyway, she had come back from hunting with a bucket of squirrels and said it was the only thing she could get her hands on to hit him with." Maggie shrugged.

"Squirrel is good meat. I love a good squirrel pie," Bertha stated.

I cringed, and everyone shot her an odd look. Bertha wasn't known for her cooking skills, so I could imagine what her squirrel pie would taste like.

I cleared my throat. "So, Linda hit Louie first?"

Maggie nodded. "And he threw a gallon of rocky road ice cream and beamed her in the head as she was running away."

The story was getting weirder and weirder by the second.

"Anyway, I think we need to add Linda as a suspect because she said when she saw Louie again, she was going to end him."

Everyone looked at each other.

I reached for the dry-erase marker. "We need to come up with a name for Linda."

Weenie raised her hand.

"What do you think, Weenie? Do you have a name for Linda?"

She shoved her glasses up on the bridge of her nose. "Well, since she was carrying dead squirrels, I suggest we call her Shoo Fly. You know, for flies on dead animals."

Bertha snorted. "You don't get flies in the winter, Weenie."

I glared at Bertha. "Maybe not, but it's a good name. We'll call Linda Shoo Fly." Without waiting on the others' opinion, I turned and wrote the name down.

CHAPTER 11

*W*e were just getting ready to leave the quilt shop when Dean pulled up. He got out, and everyone waited to see what news he brought.

"Hello, ladies," he greeted everyone.

"Enough with the pleasantries, Dean. Are you here to arrest poor Weenie?" Bertha belted out.

Dean grimaced. "I'm here to let Weenie know she can go back to her home if she wants to. The crime scene has been processed."

Weenie smiled slightly. "Thanks, Dean. It will be good to sleep in my own bed tonight."

Mom touched Weenie's arm. "Honey, are you sure you want to be alone tonight?"

Agnes shivered. "What if Louie's ghost shows up while you are there alone tonight?"

I shot Agnes a look, but she didn't notice.

"I don't believe in ghosts." Elizabeth rolled her eyes. "Once you are dead, you are dead."

Bertha frowned. "I don't know about that, Elizabeth. I've seen some weird things. Things I can't explain."

Agnes snorted. "Probably one of your dead husbands coming back for vengeance."

Bertha glared and shoved her finger in Agnes's face. "Don't disrespect the paranormal."

I sighed. "Enough. Let's not scare Weenie."

Weenie blinked behind her glasses. "I'm not scared, Dove. Louie's dead. He can't hurt me anymore." She lightly touched her arm where I had seen the bruises from his fingerprints. She walked down the steps of the shop and went to Bertha's van to wait for her to unlock the door.

The ladies scattered to their own vehicles, leaving me and Dean alone.

"That was a weird thing for Weenie to say." Dean rubbed the back of his head.

I bit my lip. He was right, but I didn't want to cast any more suspicion on Weenie than necessary. Instead, I changed the subject. "So any new information on the case?"

Dean sighed heavily. "We found Louie's truck. He parked it in the woods off an old trail and walked through the woods to her house. The question is why was he going to Weenie's." His brow furrowed, deep in thought."

I huffed. "Sounds like he wasn't up to any good." I crossed my arms over my chest.

"Have you conjured up any more suspects?" He grinned.

I brightened. "Actually, I have. Linda Martinez. Apparently, Louie hit her in the back of the head with a gallon of rocky road."

He narrowed his eyes. "Rocky road ice cream?"

I nodded.

"Why did he do that?"

I knew I was going to regret the next few words out of my mouth. "Because she hit him in the head with a bucket of dead squirrels."

Dean stood there unspeaking.

"It's weird. I know. They got into an argument about him raising her rent. Just investigate her." I shrugged and walked off, leaving him staring after me.

CHAPTER 12

$\mathcal{T}$hat night, my phone buzzed, jerking me awake out of dead sleep.

I thrust my arm from under the mountain of quilts and reached for my phone. The electricity was back on at our house but the temps were still freezing so I kept the pile of quilts on my bed for warmth.

"Hello?"

There was a beat of silence before I heard a small voice. "Dove, I'm scared."

I sat up in bed and glanced at the clock on my bedside table. "Who is this?" It was one o'clock.

"It's Weenie. I keep hearing noises at my front door. Sounds like someone banging."

I frowned and threw my legs over the side of the bed. "You need to call 911. The cops can get out there faster than I can." I hissed as my bare feet padded on the cold hardwood floor.

"I don't want to hang up, Dove. What if you're the last person I speak to before I get killed?"

I knocked on Mom's door before entering. She slowly opened her eyes and looked at me.

"Look, Weenie. I'm getting Mom to call 911. Stay on the phone with me."

My mom's eyes grew wide. "What's going on, Dove?"

I covered the phone with my hand. "Weenie says she is hearing noises on her front porch. Call 911 and tell them to get a car out there. I'm going to drive over there while I stay on the phone with her."

Mom didn't utter a word but did as I asked.

"Weenie, I'm on my way." I hurried to my room.

"Don't take too long, Dove. People can be murdered in minutes."

My heart was in my chest as I hurriedly threw on some clothes. "I'm hurrying." I grabbed my coat and car keys before hurrying down the stairs.

"Hurry, Dove." Weenie whispered.

I slid into the car and started the engine. "Can you see anyone on the front porch?"

I backed out of the driveway. The roads had iced over again once the sun went down, and the temps dropped. I felt the car slip on the driveway a bit and eased off the gas.

I slowly drove down the street, white-knuckling the steering wheel.

"Weenie, are you still there?" I put the phone on speaker and set it on the passenger seat.

"I am still in my bedroom. I'm too scared to leave my room to see who's outside."

I turned onto the next street. "That's okay. Lock your door. Just in case."

My heart was about to beat out of my chest as I drove as safely as I could to get to Weenie.

"My door is locked," Weenie said quietly.

"Is there any way you can shove something against the door?" I turned onto the road heading to Weenie's house.

"Hang on. I think I can move the dresser over."

The next thing I heard was the sound of furniture scraping across the hardwood floor.

"I'm almost there, Weenie." My headlights bobbed on her mailbox.

I drove up the driveway. My heart dropped in my chest when I realized I had beat the police out here.

"Dang." I gritted out between my teeth.

"What is it, Dove?" The fear in Weenie's voice was rising.

"Nothing." I cleared my throat and parked. "It seems like I beat the police. I'm in front of your house." I turned the car off and sat.

"Do you see anything?"

I scanned the porch but couldn't make out anything beyond shadows.

"Stay in the house. I'll come to you." I grabbed my phone and reached for the door handle. I opened it and braced myself as I stepped outside.

The wind was bitter against my face and my hands were trembling with fear. I tried to snuggle down deep in my white coat, but the cold fear went deep into my bones.

I quickly turned on the flashlight app on my phone and shone it on the porch. The shadows lengthened, and I strained to hear any approaching sirens.

A branch snapped behind me.

I screamed and spun around. I shone my phone in that direction and searched for anything that moved.

"Hello?" I called out.

A twig snapped. My heart pounded. "The police are on their way." I called out, hoping that would be enough to scare off someone.

I was alone outside with no weapon of any kind to defend myself.

"I should have waited in the car." I muttered to myself.

"What's going on out there, Dove?" Weenie asked.

I jumped when I heard her voice. I had forgotten I was still on the phone with her.

"I thought I heard something." I started for the porch.

"Do you see anything at the door? Sounded like a demon trying to scrape his way inside."

I swallowed the lump in my throat. "Weenie, did you have to describe it quite like that?"

I stepped to the porch and turned to the right. I saw nothing.

Suddenly, something rammed into my back, knocking me flat on my stomach. I felt hot breath against my neck.

I was paralyzed in fear. I couldn't move. I couldn't even breathe. It was the demon!

With a whine of sirens, a patrol car came barreling up the driveway. Whatever evil entity was breathing on my neck suddenly left.

The police car stopped, and a figure jumped out, shining a light in my face. "Don't move. Put your hands up!"

Now I was seized by a different kind of fear. Staying on my stomach, I lifted my hands in the air.

The front door opened, and Weenie stepped outside. "What are you doing on the ground, Dove? It's freezing out here."

"Ma'am. Please stay inside until we get the intruder hand-cuffed." The officer approached with his gun still aimed at me.

Weenie glanced back down at me. "Dove isn't the intruder. I called her to come over."

I held my breath as the officer reached me. He shone his flashlight in my face, and I squinted.

"Dove? You're Dean's girlfriend, aren't you?"

I slowly got to my feet and shot him a look.

He had enough sense to give me a sheepish look. "Sorry, ma'am. I hope Dean won't get upset with me about this."

I brushed the snow off my jeans and then looked at him. I could tell from his heavy New York accent he wasn't from around these parts. I wanted to be angry, but he looked like he had just graduated from the police academy straight out of high school, so I didn't have it in me.

"Don't worry about it. My name is Dove Agnew. You must be new in Harland Creek."

He nodded. "Yes ma'am. I'm Bryson Nicolas."

I looked over at Weenie who was peeking out from behind her front door. She'd stepped back inside because of the cold. "Are you okay, Weenie?"

She blinked and looked around nervously. "I'm okay. Did you see who was on my porch?

I shook my head. "No. But I did hear something near the woods before something knocked me on the ground."

Her eyes widened. "Did it sound like a ghost?"

I glanced over at the officer, who was listening raptly and writing down everything I was saying.

"No, it sounded like branches snapping. Like maybe someone walking. Then something knocked me to the ground." I nodded toward the porch. "Bryson, maybe you should look on the porch for any footsteps. You may find some in the snow."

His face brightened. "That's a good idea." He hurried toward the steps as I rolled my eyes.

Another set of flashing lights came up the driveway, and I knew from the sound of the engine that it was Dean.

I shoved my hands into my coat pockets and made my way over to him.

He got out of the vehicle with Tarzan beside him.

"Dove, what are you doing here?" He frowned.

"Weenie called me. I'm the one who told Mom to call 911. Weenie was scared to death." I glanced back at the house. "She said she heard someone on the porch trying to get in. When I got here, I didn't see anyone, but I heard someone moving around near the woods and then something knocked me down once I got on the porch."

His eyes widened. "Are you okay?"

I nodded.

Dean pulled out his flashlight and shone it toward the woods.

Bryson jogged toward us. "Dean, I'm sorry for trying to arrest Dove. I really didn't know she wasn't the intruder." He looked at Dean with a pained look.

Dean glared at him and then looked at me. "Did he pull a gun on you?"

I shrugged and wished Bryson had kept his mouth shut. "I'm fine, Dean. Besides, it was dark, and he wasn't expecting me to be here."

Dean shot the new police officer a death look. "We'll talk about this back at the station."

I cleared my throat. "Bryson, did you find any footprints on the porch?"

He looked at me and nodded. "I found some smaller prints that may be yours. And another set, which look odd."

Dean cocked his head. "Let's go have a look."

I followed the two men up the steps. Dean shone his light on the snow-covered porch. I saw my own set of footsteps near the door.

I squinted and pointed. "What's that?"

Dean knelt and studied the disturbed snow leading off to the left of the porch.

"That's odd. It looks like more than one set of prints that lead away from the door. They are hard to make out, and it looks like there was some shuffling going on." He looked at me. "Probably heard you pulling into the driveway and took off."

He stood and followed the pattern of disturbed snow to the end of the porch. "And it looks like whoever was here jumped over the railing. I bet whoever it was ran off into the woods."

I grabbed his arm. Tarzan growled.

"Do you think Tarzan smells them? Are they still here?" I was beginning to think venturing out here at night by myself was a terrible idea.

Dean walked down the steps into the yard. "Tarzan, seek!"

The German shepherd wasted no time and headed to the side of the house. He put his nose to the ground and picked up a scent. Within seconds he was running into the woods with Dean and Bryson behind him.

Shivers went down my spine as they left me standing there alone. I turned and hurried back up the steps and knocked on Weenie's door. "Weenie, it's me. Open the door."

She cracked the door and then opened it all the way when she spotted me standing there alone.

"I'm coming inside." I didn't wait for an invitation and stepped inside. I quickly shut the door behind me.

The electricity was still off. Weenie had half a dozen candles lit in the living room, along with a blazing fire in the fireplace. If the circumstances weren't so spooky, the ambience would be quite romantic.

"Did they find someone, Dove?" Weenie looked more worried than scared.

"Tarzan picked up a scent, and they are in the woods right now. "

She shook her head. "That's the one thing about living out in the country by myself. I don't have any close neighbors when something like this happens."

I bit my lip. "Would you feel safer if you came and spent the night with us? We would love to have you. Besides we he have electricity."

Weenie gave me a sad smile. "No, thank you, Dove. I've lived this long by myself. No point in getting afraid now." She frowned. "Too bad that Petunia is missing. I would ask Elizabeth if I could keep her with me. She would make a good guard goat."

I chuckled at the thought of the goat being a good protector. "You're probably right. She's not afraid of anything." I swallowed hard.

"I hope she is okay. It's gotten cold these last few nights. I hate to think about her being cold and all alone."

I shoved away those thoughts and walked over to the window to peer out. I could still see the play of Dean's flashlight. "Petunia is smart. I'm sure she is safe in someone's barn.

Weenie gave me an uneasy look. "I hope you're right. But the world isn't the safe place that it once was. There's just too much bad in it."

CHAPTER 13

*W*eenie's door opened, and we both turned to see Dean and Tarzan. They stepped inside.

I notice the look on Dean's face—like he was trying to conceal a secret.

"What did you find?" I asked.

"Found this in the woods." He held up a red scarf in his hand.

"So, there was someone on the front porch." The words spilled out before I could catch them. I spun around to look at Weenie's face.

Her brow narrowed in worry. She clasped her hands together tightly.

"I think I should stay here tonight." I spoke up.

Dean grimaced. "Dove, I don't think either of you should be out here alone."

I looked back at Weenie. She said nothing.

"I know, Dean. But Weenie wants to spend the night in her own bed. And I would feel better if I stayed with her. That is, if you don't mind me imposing, Weenie." I looked over at her.

Weenie's shoulders relaxed, and I could tell she was relieved I offered.

"That would be lovely Dove. You can stay in the guest bedroom. It's down the hall to the left. I'll just make sure everything is tidy." Weenie grabbed a candle and headed down the hall.

"Dove, I don't think you two should stay here. What if whoever tried to get inside comes back?"

I tried desperately to shove that thought away. The truth was I didn't want to stay there. But I knew Weenie wasn't going to leave her home. And I also knew I couldn't let her stay by herself. I glanced down at Tarzan.

When I looked up at Dean, a slow smile settled across my face. "What if Tarzan stays with me?"

Dean frowned. "Here? Overnight?"

I sighed. "Yes. Look I know we've had problems getting along in the past, but I think he'll be fine. Besides, it seems like his issue is really with Petunia."

Dean shook his head. "I don't know. I don't think that's a good idea."

I shrugged. "Well, either he stays with us, or we will be staying alone."

Dean studied me for a beat and then bent down to Tarzan's level. "I need you to spend the night with Dove, okay? I'll pick you up first thing in the morning." He gave the dog a rub on the head and stood to face me. "Dove, call me if you need me." He glanced around. "I have half a mind to stay with you."

I laughed and shook my head. "No, Dean. You probably won't get any sleep here. Besides, Weenie will probably make you sleep on the couch." I eyed the antique furniture. "And it doesn't look like it would make for a good night's sleep."

He stared at me for a beat and then pulled me in for a kiss.

Tarzan, feeling left out, nuzzled his way between us and let out a bark.

"Fine, Tarzan." Dean sighed heavily. "Make sure you lock this behind me." He walked to the front door and closed it behind him softly.

Weenie appeared with a candle in her hand. "Your room is ready, Dove."

I forced a smile. "Thanks. Tarzan is going to spend the night too. I think I might sit up for a while. I don't think I can sleep right now." Tarzan curled up beside the fireplace.

Her shoulders slumped with relief. "Oh, I'm so glad you said that. I'm about to jump out of my skin. Why don't I make us a cup of hot tea and we'll sit by the fire?"

I nodded. "That sounds good. But let me fix it."

She shook her head adamantly. "Absolutely not. This is the least I can do. Besides, it feels good to have a task to keep my hands busy. Keeps my mind off unpleasant things."

I didn't argue. I eased into the plush, worn armchair beside the fireplace and looked at Tarzan.

"Come here, boy." I pointed to the floor beside my feet.

Tarzan cocked his head.

"Sit, Tarzan." I commanded.

The dog eased over to the fireplace and sat down.

"You can lie down." When he didn't do it anyway, I lowered my hand to the floor, hoping the canine would understand me.

Shockingly enough, Tarzan did! He curled up into a ball and laid down.

"I made chamomile tea, Dove. It always helps me sleep." Weenie walked in with two cups of tea in delicate China cups. She handed one to me before sitting in the other chair across from me.

"Thank you, Weenie." I took a sip and sighed.

The old woman's house, nestled deep in the countryside,

exuded an eerie yet comforting charm. The flames crackled softly, casting dancing shadows across the room filled with old photographs and antiques. I glanced at the photos, realizing most of them were of Weenie and the quilting ladies. I wondered if Weenie had ever regretted not marrying.

"Thank you for staying with me, Dove," said Weenie, her voice trembling slightly. She set her teacup down and grabbed a knitted shawl from the back of the chair and draped it across her shoulders.

"Thanks for letting me stay. I don't think I've been in your house very often. It's very charming."

Weenie smiled and picked up her cup. "Thank you. It was my mother's house. I've always felt safe here." Worried lines creased her forehead. "Not so much now."

My heart tugged for her. "After this case is solved, you'll feel safe again, Weenie."

She gave me a tiny smile. "I feel much safer with you here."

I smiled reassuringly. "I'm glad. I hope you don't mind that Tarzan is spending the night as well. Dean insisted."

Weenie glanced down at Tarzan, whose eyes were slowly drifting shut. "I'm glad Tarzan is here. He's such a sweet dog. I love it when he gives me kisses."

My smile dropped. "Tarzan gives you kisses?"

She nodded. "Of course. But maybe that's because I always have a treat in my purse for him."

I snorted. "He's never given me kisses. He always gives me a hard time."

Weenie looked at me and blinked behind her large glasses. "Try carrying some beef jerky in your purse."

I just rolled my eyes, knowing she couldn't see my expression in the dark.

A sudden gust of wind rattled the windows, making both of us glance toward the darkness outside. I glanced at

Tarzan, who only opened his eyes slightly and didn't make a sound.

If Tarzan didn't sense danger, then we were okay.

My mind wandered to the red scarf found earlier. I tried remembering if I had seen it before on someone in town. But my mind came up blank.

"Tell me more about what you heard before you called me," I prompted gently.

Weenie's brow furrowed as she recalled the events. "It was around midnight. I heard fast footsteps crunching in the snow, and then a thud against the side of the house. At first, I thought I had dreamed it. But I got out of bed, and I peeked out the window, and that's when I saw a shadow moving between the trees. It was too dark to see anything clearly, and that's when I called..." her voice faltered.

I nodded, encouraging her to continue. "I saw the look on your face. You recognized the scarf that Dean found?"

Weenie hesitated, then sighed. "Yes, it belonged to my mother. I kept it in a trunk in the attic. I don't know how it ended up out there."

A chill ran down my spine. "Do you think someone's been in the house?"

"I don't know," Weenie admitted, her eyes wide with worry. "But it's possible."

I set her teacup down and stood up. "Do you mind if I check the attic?"

Weenie shook her head. "Are you sure you want to check now? You could wait until the morning."

I had to know right away. I couldn't go to sleep unless I was sure there was no one else in the house. "I'll go now." I stood and looked at the sleeping dog. "Tarzan, come."

Tarzan lifted his head and followed me. Weenie pointed out the stairs leading to the attic and waited for us at the bottom. "The scarf was in the ornate trunk in the corner of the attic. It's impossible to miss."

Together, Tarzan and I ascended the creaky wooden stairs. I held my phone with the flashlight app as we climbed each step until we reached the top. The attic door groaned open, revealing a dusty space filled with old trunks and forgotten memories. I let Tarzan walk in first, watching him sniff and investigate before I stepped inside.

I spotted a large fancy trunk in the corner. I approached the trunk cautiously and opened it. Inside, neatly folded clothes and keepsakes lay undisturbed, except for one glaring absence. There was a dusty outline where the scarf had been.

"Whoever took the scarf must have a key or know a way in," I muttered to Tarzan, who poked his head in the trunk.

I closed the trunk and looked around the attic. I could not see a second way into the attic.

As we made our way back downstairs, Weenie stared up at us. "Did you find anything?"

I shook my head. "I saw the outline where the scarf had been in the trunk. We looked around, and there is no way they could have gotten in through the attic."

Weenie blinked. "Which means they came through my door. Just like Louie did."

I nodded. "So they probably came in while you were spending the night at our house."

Weenie bit her lip. I grabbed her hand and gave it a reassuring squeeze. "Don't worry, Weenie. We will get to the bottom of this. You'll get your peace of mind back. I promise."

She said nothing but walked back to the living room, where we settled into our chairs.

The wind howled outside, but inside, the warmth of the fire and the determination to help Weenie kept the cold at bay.

CHAPTER 14

I woke up the next day feeling unusually warm and cozy. When I opened my eyes, I saw the reason why. Tarzan had curled up against me during the night and was currently snoring away.

I smiled and let out a yawn. When I did, a white cloud came out of my mouth, reminding me the heat was still off.

I eased out from under the weight of Tarzan and placed my feet on the floor. Tarzan lifted his head when I moved but quickly went back to sleep, clearly uninterested in getting out of bed.

I grimaced, reached for a quilt hanging off the foot of the bed, and wrapped it around my shoulders for warmth. The cold floor leached any warmth in my feet through my socks with each step I took toward the kitchen.

When I got there, I froze. "Weenie, what are you doing up?"

She was sitting at the kitchen table with her hands around a cup of coffee and her hair sticking up every which way.

"I tossed and turned all night. Finally, I just got up." She pointed to the coffee pot. "There's a fresh pot, Dove. Help yourself." She looked behind me. "Where's Tarzan?"

I poured myself a cup. "He's sleeping in." Heading to the kitchen table, I sat down. I took a sip of the coffee and sighed. "I think I'm going to go back to the RV park and see if I can talk to Linda Martinez."

Weenie blinked. "Isn't Dean going to question her?"

I shrugged. "Probably. But I want to talk to her myself. Women usually open to me. Besides, while I'm there, I'll see what Polly is up to. Might as well question them both if the opportunity presents itself."

Weenie nodded. "Keep an eye out for Petunia. Maybe you will get lucky and find her."

I gave Weenie a sad smile. "Maybe."

After I finished my coffee, I took Tarzan outside so he could do his business. When he was done, he glanced back toward the wooded area and let out a small growl, as if he was remembering last night's events.

I said my goodbyes to Weenie and loaded Tarzan up in the car. I was halfway down the driveway when I met Dean. We both stopped, and he got out of his car. I rolled down my window, and he smiled when Tarzan crawled into my lap to give Dean kisses.

"Get off." I muttered against the dog's fur.

Dean laughed and rubbed Tarzan's head before walking to the passenger side and opening the door. Tarzan jumped out and Dean got in. "I take it you two got on last night?" Tarzan crawled into Dean's lap and looked out the front window.

"I did appreciate how warm he kept me." I admitted.

Dean nodded. "He's great to snuggle with on a cold winter's night." He looked at me. "Speaking of last night, you could have gotten yourself killed."

I glanced away. "You mean one of your inexperienced officers could have killed me."

Dean's smile slid off his face. "I had a talk with Bryson."

I knew that look. When Dean had one of his serious expressions, he meant business. "There was no harm done. He's young, he didn't mean any harm. What's someone from New York doing down in Mississippi, anyway? He seems like a fish out of water."

Dean snorted. "He wanted to transfer some place where the crime rate was low. From his paperwork, he doesn't seem to think very fast on his feet. And his superiors thought a small-town atmosphere would be a better fit for him."

It was my turn to snort. "Crime rate low? Apparently, they haven't seen our sudden bump in murders in our small town."

Dean gave me a blank stare. "So, what do you have on your schedule today?"

I pressed my lips together and debated what exactly I should tell my chief-of-police boyfriend.

"I need to look for Petunia," I stated. It wasn't exactly a lie. I would certainly be looking for the little goat while I was out investigating this murder.

Dean studied me for a minute. "Well, then, don't let me keep you. Just make sure you are careful on the road. Some spots are still slippery." He kissed my forehead before slipping out of the car with Tarzan.

I waited while Dean backed out of the drive before putting my car in gear.

CHAPTER 15

$\mathcal{M}$y stomach rumbled as I headed to the Chateau RV Park, reminding me I should have eaten breakfast before I left. Hopefully the donut shop was open, and I could stop by after talking to Polly and Linda.

I pulled up to Polly's RV and killed the engine. Her car was there, so I knew she was home.

Opening the door, I slid out of my car and walked up to the RV. I heard raised voices coming from inside. I pressed my ear to the door to hear what was being said.

Suddenly the floor flew open, pushing me backward to the ground. I landed with a thud on my back.

I squeezed my eyes shut against the pain shooting through my chest.

"What the heck are you doing here?" A scrawny woman with black hair and blonde highlights stood over me, glaring.

I guessed her to be Linda.

"Linda, you've killed her!" Polly ran to my side and knelt. "Dove? Are you okay?"

I eased up on my elbows and finally caught my breath that the fall had knocked out of me.

"I think I'm okay. Thanks for your concern." I shot a look at Linda.

She propped her hands on her hips and snorted. "That's what you get for being so dang nosy." She glanced over at Polly and pointed a finger at her. "And as for you, I would watch my back if I were you."

Linda strode off toward a small vintage camper that had seen better days.

I got my feet under me and stood. "Well, she's pleasant, isn't she?"

Polly's face went white. "I've never met anyone like her. She's awfully mean." She looked me over and then frowned. "What are you doing here, Dove?"

I gave her a small smile. "I came to see how you were doing after Louie's death. I know you two were… close."

Her eyes darted around as if making sure no one was watching us. "Why don't we go inside where it's warm."

I followed her up the stairs of the RV and closed the door behind me.

"Can I get you some coffee? I have some day-old donuts too."

I brightened at the mention of the sugary treat. It was well-known fact donuts were my weakness.

"That would be great. Thanks." I eased into the worn brown sofa and looked around. Her laptop was open on the kitchen table with papers and books piled around it. The trashcan by the kitchen sink was overflowing with paper plates and a mountain of clothes were piled on the passenger seat.

"Sorry the place is such a mess." Polly's face went red as she handed me the coffee and glazed donut wrapped in a paper towel. She sat down with her own cup of coffee.

"I understand that things get a little messy when traveling." I took a bite of the donut and sighed as I chewed.

"Thanks for the donut. I didn't have time to grab breakfast." I nodded toward her laptop. "I was going to ask has your new book come out. Some of the quilting ladies were asking about it."

Polly looked at me from over the rim of her coffee cup. "It's proving more difficult to write than I originally thought. I am having a bit of writer's block." She looked at the ground.

I set my coffee down on the small table beside me. "Polly, I'm sorry about Louie."

Something flashed across her eyes. "Yes. Well, we had been out of touch for the past few months."

Interesting. "Really? Were you coming back to Harland Creek to rekindle your...friendship?"

Her face went red. "I wouldn't exactly say that." She swallowed and didn't meet my gaze.

I wanted to know more, but I didn't want to push.

"Truth is, I ran out of money. I gave Louie some money before I left. He said he was going to invest it and make me some money. When my ex-husband fell behind on my alimony, I called Louie to get my money back. He said that he lost it in the investment. I told him I wanted my money back, and I needed it back ASAP. He stopped taking my calls, so I decided to drive down here. We had an argument the day before he died when he told me he wasn't going to give my money back to me." She shook her head. "I've never seen him so angry." She looked at me. "Dove, I know Louie had a bad reputation, but he never was angry or mean to me. Until the other day. There was a darkness in his eyes when he yelled at me. He even threatened me if I didn't drop it."

My mouth gaped. "He threatened you. What did he say?"

She pressed her lips together and then took a deep breath.

"He said if I didn't shut up about the money, he would shut me up."

I shook my head. "I'm so sorry, Polly."

She dabbed at her eyes. "I was a fool for my ex-husband, and I swore that I never would be a fool again. I swore that I wouldn't let another man take advantage of me. I guess I was wrong. After he threatened me, I swore I would make Louie pay."

My face must have shown my surprise. "Polly, what did you do?"

She lifted her chin. "I called my attorney to see what could be done. He sent him a legal notice that he better pay up or I was suing."

I nodded and relaxed back in my seat. "So, what was Linda doing over here? Are you two friends?"

Polly's face darkened. "Friends? With that snake? Absolutely not. You know she had gotten into a fight with Louie before he died. She might be a woman, but she's a dangerous woman."

I nodded my head in agreement and stood. "Thank you for the coffee and the donut. It was much appreciated." I headed to the kitchen and placed my cup in the overflowing sink. I noticed an overdue bill by the coffee pot. It seems Polly really had fallen on hard times.

I gave her a grateful smile. "I hope you get your book done soon. I'm sure it's going to be a hit."

Polly snorted. "I hope so. Or else I'll be completely broke."

I saw myself out and got in my car. I slowly drove around the RV park looking for any signs of Linda. I finally spotted her huddled over an in-ground BBQ pit.

I parked and got out of my car. She looked up before I got halfway to her and sneered. "What do you want?"

I lifted my chin and tried to appear brave as I walked

toward her. "I'm here to talk to you about Louie. I heard you guys got into a physical altercation before he died."

She glared and rubbed the back of her head. "Louie always was a horrible human being. I can't say that anyone will miss him." She snorted. "Well maybe Polly. But she did always have bad taste in men."

I frowned. "Did you know Polly before she came to Harland Creek?"

Linda growled. "No. It's common knowledge that her husband left her for another woman. Then she tries to start a relationship with Louie. She's a fool thinking that man cared anything about her other than what little money she had left." She lifted her chin. "I never would trust a man to do what he says he's going to do."

I cocked my head. "Can you tell me where you were on the day Louie was murdered?"

She looked at me and let out a laugh. "Who do you think you are? The cops?"

I narrowed my eyes. "No. Just a concerned citizen."

She snorted and glared at me. "Well for your information, I was in the woods, hunting for squirrels." She grew serious. "My last batch got messed up."

I arched a brow. "They got messed up when you threw them at Louie."

She glared and took a step near me. "I'm going to tell you like I told Dean Gray. If I were you, I would look at the person who was the closet to him."

I blinked. "Polly."

She let out a laugh that sent shivers up my spine. "No, you dummy. The guy who worked for Louie. Donnie Rae Davis. If you think he was mean to me, you should see how much worse he treated Donnie Rae." With that she turned on her heel and headed inside her camper.

CHAPTER 16

 y phone rang when I pulled out of the Chateau RV Park. I quickly answered when I saw it was Mom.

"Hey, what's up?" I was grateful the temps were higher today and a lot of the ice from the roads were starting to melt.

"Petunia has been sighted!" Mom's voice brimmed with hope and excitement.

"Where?"

"Sloan has a deer camera set up on his hunting land. When he reviewed the footage, there was a picture of Petunia with a herd of deer."

My eyes widened. "When was the photo taken?" I pulled off the side of the road.

"Last night, around three a.m. Sloan has been looking for her on his four-wheeler."

I frowned. "I should go help. She may not go to someone she doesn't know. Send me directions to his land."

I waited until Mom sent me the directions before turning my car around and following the directions.

"Does Elizabeth know?"

Mom sighed heavily. "She does. Agnes has been trying to get her to stay home, but she is insisting on going out to that land to search for herself. Maybe if she sees you out there, she won't go into the woods herself. The last thing we need is her falling and having to have another hip replacement. It took her forever to get back to full health after the last surgery."

I nodded. "I'll talk her out of it. I'm almost there. I'll keep you updated."

I pulled off the main road to a dirt road. I spotted a car and two trucks pulled off the side of the road up ahead.

When I saw Elizabeth and Agnes in a heated debate, I knew I was at the right place.

I parked and got out of the car. "Hey what are you two arguing about?" I called out as I approached.

Agnes sighed heavily and parked her hands on her hips. "I'm glad you are here, Dove. I'm trying to talk some sense in this old woman. She thinks she's going to go traipsing in the woods to find Petunia. Heather, Grayson, and Sloan are already in the woods calling for her. There is no need for Elizabeth to go in there as well."

Elizabeth glared at me.

"Agnes is right. You really don't need to go in there." I looked over their shoulders. "How long have the others been in the woods?"

"About ten minutes. They said they are following a small deer trail in there. Sloan said to watch out for icy patches. The sun hasn't reached through the trees to melt anything yet," Agnes said.

I nodded and pulled my gloves out of my coat pocket. Sliding the gloves on my hands, I had a moment of regret for buying a white coat.

"I have my phone. If I find anything, I'll call."

Elizabeth grabbed my arm as I was turning to leave. "Dove. I don't understand why Petunia ran off in the first place. She was loved. What if she doesn't want to come home?"

I saw the hurt in her eyes and gave her a comforting smile. "I'm sure she is trying to get home. She probably just got turned around."

Agnes snorted. "I think she's having the time of her life running around with some wild animals."

Elizabeth narrowed her eyes. "You act like she's on spring break."

Agnes shrugged. "Maybe she is. Imagine the stories she will have once she gets home."

I wanted to remind the old women that Petunia was a goat and couldn't talk. But I didn't want to burst their bubble. Instead, I smiled and headed into the woods.

CHAPTER 17

I grimaced as I tore my white coat free from yet another branch. I had tried to be careful walking down the small trail, but the thorny branches were so close together it was impossible to walk through them without getting snagged.

"Dove?"

I looked up and spotted Heather walking toward me. I gave a quick wave and tugged my coat sleeve free.

"What are you doing here?" Heather's eyes were red from crying. Petunia was like a child to her.

"Mom called and told me Petunia was spotted. She said Elizabeth and Agnes drove over here and wanted me to make sure Elizabeth didn't try to walk out in the woods."

Heather's eyes widened. "I didn't know they were coming. I called and told her about Petunia but didn't expect her to show up. It's too cold for her to be out here."

I nodded. "I know. She's with Agnes. I promised her I would walk and see if I could find Petunia."

Heather gave me a sad smile. "Thanks, Dove. Petunia sure

loves you, especially after all the time you two spent together."

I shoved my hands in my coat pocket. "She's a special little goat. And she's tough. I'm sure she's fine. Where are Sloan and Grayson?"

She nodded over her shoulder. "Back up there. It's a short walk. They are trying to judge which way she went from the deer camera. It's hard to tell the difference between her tracks and the deer tracks."

I followed her back the way she came until we ran up on the two guys, who were studying the ground.

"Dove, what are you doing here?" Sloan frowned.

"I heard about Petunia. I'm here to help look. Do you have an idea which way she went?"

Sloan pulled out his phone. "Well, according to the video on my phone, she headed west." He pointed.

"So, she is headed toward town." I cocked my head.

"Looks that way," Sloan stated. "But I think I'm going to check west, just in case she changed her mind."

"Thanks, Sloan," Grayson said. He held out his hand to Heather. "Come on. Let's go see if we can find our naughty goat."

I watched as Heather and Grayson headed off in the direction that Petunia was last spotted.

Sloan started to head west when I grabbed his arm. "Sloan, wait. I want to ask you something."

He turned. "Okay."

I bit my lip and then proceeded. "Have you interviewed Donnie Rae regarding Louie's death?"

Sloan's eyes narrowed on me. "Why would you ask that? You're not supposed to be looking into this case, Dove."

I lifted my chin. "When is it a crime to give suggestions about a case?"

Sloan studied me. He crossed his arms over his chest. "For

your information, we did try to talk to Donnie Rae but he's been out of town. He's supposed to be back soon."

My eyes went wide. "What exactly did he do for Louie?"

Sloan shrugged. "He worked as a handyman for Louie. He took care of repairs on all his rental properties. Louie treated him horribly and paid him next to. nothing."

I cringed. "So why didn't Donnie Rae leave and work somewhere else?"

Sloan rolled his eyes. "Because Donnie Rae didn't finish high school. After his father died, he had to become the man in the family he had to find work. He worked for Gertrude first before she died. When Louie took over, he cut Donnie Rae's pay. Donnie Rae started looking for work. He got hired by Farmer Brown doing part time work about a month ago."

I bit my lip. "That must have made Louie angry."

Sloan eyed me. "Sure did. In fact, they came to blows over it last week. We have witnesses that saw Louie hit Donnie Rae and knock him to the ground."

My stomach dropped. "That's a pretty good reason for wanting to kill Louie. But I guess we won't hear Donnie Rae's side of the story until you find him and question him."

Sloan sighed. "Right now, we have a goat to find. Can we please go look for Petunia? This is my first day off in a while, and I don't want to waste it talking about Louie."

I shook my head. "Fine. Let's go."

We made it about twenty feet into the woods before Sloan stopped. "We can't go any farther because the woods are too thick. And you have just about ruined your white coat. You should have worn something else."

I glanced down at the dirt-stained coat I'd been so proud of. The melting snow from the tree branches had bled into the white wool.

I gritted my teeth instead of telling Sloan to mind his business where my fashion sense was concerned.

I heard a branch snap and turned around to see a rather large deer staring back at me.

"Son of a..." Sloan breathed out. "It's him."

His antlers were huge, and he was standing only a few feet away from me.

"Don't move, Dove. It's Big Boy. The buck I've been hunting," Sloan whispered.

I couldn't move if I wanted to. I was scared stiff. My legs felt like jelly, and my heart threatened to leap out of my chest.

The buck eyed me and snorted. White clouds billowed out of his nostrils.

"Sloan? He snorted at me. Is this a bad thing?" My voice trembled as I spoke.

"Don't move," Sloan stated again.

The big buck pawed the ground and lowered his head.

"He looks like he's going to charge me, Sloan," I spit out between my teeth.

"Be still. Don't move." Sloan warned.

Suddenly the deer lifted his head, snorted, and charged me.

I stared in horror as my gruesome death approached me.

The loud bark of a dog knocked me out of my paralysis, and I turned just in time to see Tarzan racing down the trail toward me.

Tarzan leaped for the deer, knocking me to the ground in the process. I hit the ground with a thud. I sat up in time to see Tarzan chasing the large deer back into the woods.

"Dove! Are you okay?" Dean knelt beside me.

I sighed. "I'm fine. Thanks to Tarzan." I frowned. "He'll come back, right?"

Dean glanced to the woods and gave a whistle. "Tarzan, back!"

The German shepherd came running back to Dean. He glanced over at me and huffed.

I scratched him between the ears. "Good job, Tarzan. I'll make it up to you when I go by the donut shop."

Dean grimaced. "I'm trying to keep him on a healthy diet, Dove. I don't like him eating junk food."

I arched my brow as he helped me to my feet. "Then you're really going to hate the fact that I shared my cookies with him last night."

Dean narrowed his eyes but didn't say anything.

I glanced down at my coat and sighed. "My coat is ruined."

Sloan shook his head. "I don't know why anyone would buy a white coat in the first place."

I glared. "Because it's pretty."

Sloan snorted and shook his head. "I think Petunia is long gone from these woods. We should head back."

Dean nodded in agreement.

By the time we walked back to where the cars were parked, Heather and Grayson were there speaking with Elizabeth and Agnes. When Heather saw us without Petunia, her face fell.

I knew what she was thinking. Another day without finding Petunia meant our chances were getting slimmer of ever finding the goat.

CHAPTER 18

We had all gathered in the back room of the quilt shop to go over the suspects in the murder of Louie. The scent of coffee and the hum of the space heater filled the small space, making it feel cozy despite the winter weather outside.

All the members of the quilting club were in attendance. Sylvia and Maggie were filling up their cups with coffee, while Agnes grabbed a slice of pound cake brought from the bakery. Lorraine and Donna were huddled together, talking. Bertha was scowling as she looked at her cell phone.

Weenie's knitting needles clacked as she worked on a blue scarf. She stopped and looked at Elizabeth sitting beside her in one of the white plastic chairs.

"I'm sorry about Petunia, Elizabeth. But I still have hope she'll be found." Weenie gave her friend's hand a squeeze.

Elizabeth lifted her chin and put on a brave face. "You're right, Weenie. We always must have hope."

I needed to change the subject. The tension in the room was so thick. I cleared my throat, picked up the marker, and walked to the dry-erase board. "So, we are here to discuss a new suspect."

Agnes's eyebrows shot up. "A new suspect? Who?"

I looked at her. "Donnie Rae. Louie's handyman."

Maggie leaned forward in her seat. "I also heard that Louie hit him a few days before Louie was found dead."

I nodded. "Maggie is right. And, according to Sloan, Donnie Rae is out of town."

Sylvia's eyebrows shot up. "Interesting."

I gave her a knowing look. "Yes. So, we need to give him a name."

Elizabeth raised her hand. "How about Bear Paw? He's a handyman, and works with his hands."

Agnes brightened. "That's a great idea. All in favor of Bear Paw, raise your hand."

Hands went up around the room, making it unanimous. I turned and wrote the name on the board.

"So far we have Crazy Quilt, who we know is innocent." I smiled at Weenie. "We also have House That Jack Built, which is Polly." I frowned. "You know, I spoke to her, and I really didn't get the feeling that she killed Louie."

Weenie cocked her head. "Why is she in town, Dove?"

I crossed my arms over my chest. "She gave Louie some money to invest. And since her writing isn't taking off like it should, she came back to get her money. Louie told her she wasn't getting it."

Mom sighed. "That's a pretty good reason to kill someone. Money is a big motivator."

I bit my lip. "Maybe. Then there is Linda Martinez, also known as Shoo Fly. I also talked to her. I could see her doing it, especially since she works for a farmer and Louie's cause of death was poisoning."

Maggie nodded. "My money is on her. She's a tough old bird and not afraid to get violent."

Sylvia nodded. "Why, just the other day she threatened to knock out my client. They got into an argument because Linda parked too close to the other woman's car. I had to make Linda go inside before she hit someone." She sighed heavily.

"You and Maggie certainly see some crazy things in your beauty shop," I stated.

Maggie snorted. "Isn't that the truth. You should hear about what happens during election years."

I shook my head. "No thanks." I pointed to the board. "Everyone keeps their eyes and ears open to see if someone drops a hint about Louie. I kind of feel like we are grasping at straws here."

Bertha snorted. "Maybe we are. Maybe it's an unsolvable murder."

Agnes harrumphed. "That's not true. It's just a hard case. That's because this is a murder that occurred during the worst time of the year. First, no one liked Louie. So, people are probably relieved he's gone. Second, it happened in a snowstorm, which probably covered the assailant's tracks and made it hard to find clues. And most importantly, people are more concerned about finding Petunia and not giving this case any more attention than necessary."

I tapped the marker to the board as I contemplated Agnes's ideas. "You are right. But right now, Weenie is still a suspect. And we are going to have to put our heads together to solve this case."

Bertha sneered. "I personally think we are all wasting our time. Since Donnie Rae left town, the police are going to try to find him. I mean, he's the most likely suspect. Who knows, maybe Linda gave Donnie Rae the poison to kill Louie. Besides, we all know Weenie didn't kill Louie."

I frowned. "I agree, Bertha. But it doesn't explain what he

was doing in her home when he died. And how in the world did he get in?"

Bertha's face went white, and her lip quivered.

"Bertha, what's wrong with you? You are white as a ghost." Agnes frowned.

Bertha shook her head. "I'm fine."

Weenie pushed her glasses up on the bridge of her nose and blinked. "You don't look fine, Bertha. Looks like you want to be sick. Is your stomach feeling queasy?

I didn't think it was possible, but Bertha went almost gray. She pressed her hand to her mouth and ran to the bathroom.

We all sat there with worried expressions until Weenie stood up. "I should go check on her."

I shook my head. "No, Weenie, I'll do it."

I headed out of the room to the bathroom down the hallway. I knocked. "Bertha."

There was a beat before Bertha snatched the door open and pulled me inside. "Dove. I did something bad."

I studied her ashen face, and then my eyes widened. "Good grief. Did you kill Louie?"

She cringed. "No, why would you say that?"

I shrugged and stuffed my hands in my pockets. "Well, I didn't mean, like, on purpose. Maybe he ate something you made." The words tumbled out before I could stop them.

I jerked my head up to her gaze, half expecting her to slap me senseless.

Instead, her eyes widened.

"Bertha? Did you kill Louie?" I gaped.

She shushed me and pressed her fingers to her lips. "No, but I did something worse. I'm the reason Louie was in Weenie's house. And she's going to disown me when she finds out." Her eyes darted around in worry.

I took a deep breath. "Calm down. You need to tell me what's going on."

Bertha braced her hands on the sink and looked down. "Louie got into Weenie's house because he overheard me telling her door combination to Larry Smith."

I blinked. "Larry? The plumber?"

Bertha nodded frantically. "Yes. The plumber. I told him to go by Weenie's house and make sure her pipes were secure for the winter weather. I knew Weenie would forget to do it. A few years ago, her pipes burst and flooded her kitchen. She had a hard time paying for what the insurance didn't cover. Anyway, I told Larry to go over there and gave him the code to her door in case she wasn't home." She looked up at me. "We were in the hardware store when we were talking. After Larry walked away, Louie stepped out into the aisle. I knew from the look on his face, that stupid smirk, that he had heard." She buried her face in her hands. "I'm a fool, and Weenie isn't going to forgive me."

I reached out and gave her arm a reassuring squeeze. "Bertha, you didn't do it on purpose. Weenie has a big heart. She will forgive you. But you need to tell her. And we need to let Dean know how Louie got into her house."

Bertha looked up and nodded slowly. "I know." She let out a large sigh. "Might as well get this over with."

I gave her a reassuring nod and followed her out of the bathroom. When we stepped into the room, all the ladies looked up at us.

"Everything okay?" Elizabeth asked.

Bertha swallowed hard and lifted her chin. "No, it's not. I have something to confess."

Agnes gasped. "Did you kill Louie, Bertha?"

Bertha grimaced. "No, Agnes." She glanced over at Weenie. "I have to confess something to Weenie."

Weenie blinked behind her large glasses. "Me? What is it, Bertha?"

Bertha took a steadying breath. "Louie got into your house because he overheard me telling Larry the code. I was only trying to get Larry to come check and make sure your pipes were wrapped up so you wouldn't have burst pipes again. I reminded you about it, but I know sometimes you get…busy and forget. Anyway, I didn't realize that Louie had heard until after it was all over." Bertha looked down at the ground. "I hope you can forgive me."

The room went silent, and Weenie slowly stood. She walked over to Bertha and took her hand. "It's not your fault Louie got into my house, Bertha. Of course I forgive you."

Bertha's eyes filled with tears at the grace Weenie showed her. "Thank you, Weenie."

The room went silent until Agnes cleared her throat.

"Can we get back to talking about this case?" Agnes grouched. "I've got to get back out there and search for Petunia."

I nodded. "I think we've covered all we know." I looked at Bertha. "Do you mind if I tell Dean how Louie got into Weenie's house?"

Bertha shook her head. "Of course not. Thanks, Dove."

After the meeting was over, I made a quick call to Dean and updated him.

CHAPTER 19

On my way home, I spotted half the Harland Creek police cars with their lights on surrounding Mac's grocery store. The entrance had been blocked off with yellow tape, and no one was allowed entrance.

I slowed my car and pulled into a parking spot away from the commotion.

Climbing out of my car, I saw Felicia Dantry leaning against the grill of her Mercedes and watching with interest. Felicia was a real estate agent and always dressed to impress.

I walked over and eyed her Christian Louboutin shoes with envy. "I love your shoes, but aren't you afraid of ruining them in this melting snow?"

Without looking at me, she cocked her head. "No woman worth her salt can ruin her designer shoes if she knows how to walk in them." She cut her eyes at me and stared at my once white wool coat. "What did you do to that amazing coat?"

I sighed and held out my arms. "I fell when I was out in the woods looking for Petunia."

She frowned. "That's too bad. But I think if you get it to

the cleaners, they might can get out the stains. I had them get some red wine stains out my white blouse."

I looked down at my coat. "I think this is more than just a few drops of red wine."

Felicia arched a brow. "It was a full glass of red wine that Tabitha threw in my face."

I gaped at her. "Tabitha did that?" I was afraid to ask what she did to warrant that action, so I didn't ask any more questions.

She looked back at the commotion at the grocery store. "It's okay. We're fine now."

I followed her gaze. "Well, that's good to know. Do you know what's going on here?"

Felicia shrugged. "I pulled in to get some dog food since we are out, and before I could get out of my car, cops showed up and blocked the entrance. I was waiting to see if there were any gunshots, but I haven't heard any."

My eyes widened. "Do you think we should move back? I mean, if there is gunfire, we might get hit."

She frowned at me. "I would have thought you would be braver than that, Dove. I mean, you are an amateur detective."

I cringed. "I wouldn't call myself a detective. It's more of a pastime, really."

Felicia grinned. "Half the town is betting that you and your old ladies will have this crime solved before the police do."

This was news to me. "Who do you have your money on?"

She grinned. "You, of course. So don't muck it up." She pushed off her Mercedes and walked to the driver's side door. "I'll grab some dog food at the hardware store." She slid behind the wheel and drove off.

I looked back toward the grocery store.

I spotted Mac, the owner, jogging toward his truck. I met him there.

"Hey, Mac. What's going on?"

Mac glared at the store. "That dang fool Donnie Rae Davis came in with a gun and took Mrs. Simpson as a hostage. He barricaded himself inside and made the rest of us leave. Said he wanted to talk to the cops and has a list of demands."

I gasped. "But Mrs. Simpson is almost eighty."

He shook his head. "She just turned ninety. And she's in a wheelchair." He mopped his head with his handkerchief. "That's probably why he took her hostage—because she can't get away from him."

I shook my head. "Why would he do that? Donnie Rae worked for Louie, right? I mean, he's never done anything like this before, has he?"

Mac shook his head. "Not that I'm aware. But it seems that the cops found out the poison that Louie died from is something that Farmer Brown keeps on his farm. The cops showed up and started asking questions. Donnie Rae was at Farmer Brown's house to talk about working full time since Louie died. Donnie Rae and Skipper didn't get along so I'm not sure if Farmer Brown would hire him full time based on that alone. Anyway, Donnie Rae took off in his car when he saw the cops. He ended up here in the grocery store, buying up a bunch of canned goods. Sloan followed him here, and when Donnie Rae saw him, he pulled out his gun from under his jacket and took Mrs. Simpson hostage." Mac pointed toward the group of police cars. "That's when the rest of the force showed up."

I frowned. "What kind of relationship did Donnie Rae and Louie have?"

Mac grunted. "Louie always had Donnie Rae under his thumb. Donnie Rae took his verbal abuse until recently."

I cocked my head. "What do you mean?"

"I saw Donnie Rae and Louie arguing about a week ago. Not sure what they were going on about, but Donnie Rae looked mad. I told Dean about it." Mac shoved his handkerchief in his pocket and crossed his arms over his chest.

"Mac, why did Donnie Rae and Skipper not get along? Was it because Skipper went to prison?"

Mac's eyebrows shot up. "No. Donnie Rae hates Skipper because Skipper is the one who killed Donnie Rae's father. Skipper was on drugs and ended up killing Donnie Rae's father in a hit and run accident. Skipper went to jail and Donnie Rae went to work with no expectation of going to college. There's been bad blood between them since."

I stared at Mac. "I had no idea."

Mac nodded. "I think it hurt Donnie Rae when Farmer Brown hired Skipper full time when he got out of prison. Donnie Rae didn't think Skipper deserved a second chance. Farmer Brown needed the help and was willing to hire him."

Suddenly there was some motion at the front of the store, and cops were moving in with weapons drawn.

"Don't do anything stupid, Donnie Rae!" Dean called out on the speaker. "Come on out, and don't hurt Mrs. Simpson."

I strained to hear what was being said but couldn't make out the words coming from inside the grocery store.

"Someone is coming out," Mac stated.

We held our breath as Donnie Rae came out, pushing Mrs. Simpson in her wheelchair with one hand while holding the gun to her with the other.

I pressed my hand to my mouth in horror.

"I can't believe Donnie Rae is treating Mrs. Simpson like that. Poor helpless thing," I said.

Mac snorted. "Mrs. Simpson may be in a wheelchair, but helpless she is not."

Suddenly, Mrs. Simpson raised what looked like an

umbrella from her lap and whacked Donnie Rae on the head. He let out a howl and pressed both hands to his head. His gun fell to the ground.

Mrs. Simpson wasn't done with him yet. She stood up from her wheelchair and rained blows down on him until he was curled up on the sidewalk, wailing like a child.

The Harland Creek police force had to physically separate her from him before taking him into custody.

"Let go of me, you dang idiots," Mrs. Simpson yelled. She drew back her umbrella and hit Sloan in the arm.

"Disarm her!" Dean yelled as he shoved Donnie Rae into the back of a patrol car.

I ran over to Dean, who looked shocked to see me there.

"Hey, I just saw everything. Is Mrs. Simpson, okay?" I glanced in the backseat, where Donnie Rae was sitting with his shoulders slumped.

Dean snorted. "I'm more worried about Sloan. She hit him hard." He turned and gave me his full attention and sobered. "She'll be fine."

I nodded. "Good. It looked scary for a minute. I thought Donnie Rae might hurt someone."

He gave me a little grin. "Hurt someone or hurt me?"

I bumped his shoulder playfully. "You know what I mean."

He turned and shouted to Sloan to get Mrs. Simpson to the police station so she could make a statement.

From the curse words coming out of her mouth, she wasn't too happy about that.

I swallowed. "Why did Donnie Rae do this?"

He leaned a hip on the car. "He took off when we were looking at the chemicals Farmer Brown keeps. We found the same pesticide that killed Louie and were taking it into evidence. He spotted us and took off before we could question him. I don't need to tell you how he incriminated himself with that alone." He nodded to the grocery. "He was planning to skip town and stopped by to pick up some water and canned goods."

I nodded. "I see."

He narrowed his eyes on me. "You have that look."

I looked back at him. "What look?"

He grimaced. "The look you get when you don't agree with who the suspect is. It's the look you give me when you go off on a tangent and investigate by yourself. It's the look that always ends up getting you in trouble."

I lifted my chin and crossed my arms over my chest. "I have no idea what you are talking about."

Dean opened his mouth to argue, but Bryson ran over. "Hey, Dean. We had a call come that Petunia was spotted in the kitchen at the diner in town. She's making quite the mess."

I gave Dean a hopeful look. "She's found."

Dean nodded. "Follow Dove over there and give them some help."

Bryson cringed. "I thought Sloan would rather go, since he knows the goat. Besides, he's tired of dealing with Mrs. Simpson. I mean, I don't think this is really police business."

Dean narrowed his eyes. "The thing about a small town is everything is police business. Now go."

Bryson looked a bit shocked but nodded his head and hurried to his car.

Dean turned back to me. "He needs to learn that there is no small job when it comes to being a cop in a small town."

I gave him a quick kiss on the cheek and ran to my car.

CHAPTER 20

$\mathcal{I}$ pulled into an empty parking spot in front of the diner and hurried in the door. I didn't have time to wait on Bryson to catch up. I didn't want Petunia to get away again.

"Dove!" Gladys, one of the waitresses, waved to me from on top of a booth table. There were scattered dishes of burgers and fries and the daily special scattered along the floor.

I ran over to her. "Are you okay?"

She shook her head. "I have a goat phobia."

I frowned. "A what?"

Her lower lip trembled. "A goat phobia. Ever since I went to the petting zoo when I was little, I have feared goats."

I nodded slowly and realized that Bryson had just entered the diner behind me. "Did a goat bite you?"

Her eyes widened, and she shook her head. "No. It peed on me. It put its paws on the fence and peed right on my favorite dress. The smell was horrendous, and we had to throw it away. I had nightmares for weeks."

I gave her a quizzical look. "Well, Petunia's a girl. And I've never known her to pee on anyone. Although she did try to eat my hair one time, but I think that's because she was hungry, so she didn't really mean any harm."

The sound of dishes crashing to the floor, followed by a bleat, came from the kitchen.

"Is she in there by herself?" I asked.

Gladys nodded. "She must have come in when the back door to the kitchen was propped open for deliveries. She tried to paw Carl, the cook, and he sprinted out like the devil was after him. All the customers got scared and ran off. I just…froze up."

I nodded. "Why don't you come down off the table and go outside? I'll take care of Petunia."

Bryson stepped forward and held out his hand. She took it and slowly climbed down. He helped her to the door while I made my way to the double swinging doors that led into the kitchen.

Petunia lifted her head from a large pot when I entered. She had some lettuce hanging from one horn, and her face was red from the vegetable soup she'd been eating.

"Petunia. I can't believe you're here! Everyone has been worried sick about you."

The goat blinked and then let out a bleat.

"Why don't we go home?" I held out my hand.

Petunia took a step back.

"Come on, girl. It's me. You know me. Just because you've been hanging out with the wildlife doesn't mean you don't know your family."

I took a step closer, and suddenly something furry ran across my foot.

I let out a scream and jumped back.

A raccoon jumped on the cutting table with a pawful of fries. It narrowed its little eyes at me and slowly ate one of the fries.

"I'm not going to hurt you, Mr. Raccoon. I just want to get Petunia and get out of your way."

I inched forward.

"Dove! Get out of the way!" Bryson rushed into the kitchen with his gun drawn.

"Don't shoot, Bryson!"

He didn't listen but continued to aim his gun. "Raccoons carry disease. It probably has Distemper."

I put my hands on his arms to lower the gun.

The raccoon saw his chance and jumped off the table and onto Petunia's back. The goat looked offended that Bryson had aimed a gun and let out a bleat. She ran for the back door, which was still open.

"Petunia! No!" I ran for the back door, but Petunia was quicker. She ran out the door and into the woods behind the grocery store.

"That was close. That raccoon could have bitten us." Bryson gave me a satisfied smile.

I closed my fingers into fists. "I doubt that. But it doesn't matter. Because you let Petunia get away. And Dean is going to be mad."

CHAPTER 21

Bertha looked at me from across Weenie's kitchen table. I had driven straight from the diner to her house. I had already told her and Weenie about losing Petunia due to Bryson's incompetence. Thankfully, Bertha called Elizabeth and updated her. I didn't have the heart to do it. Afterwards I told them about Donnie Rae and what had happened at the grocery store.

"Donnie Rae is the killer. Looks like the police got their guy this time." Bertha smirked and sipped on her hot tea. "This case is officially closed."

Weenie stayed silent and slowly rubbed her thumb against the handle of the teacup.

"Weenie, what are you thinking?"

She looked at me with sad eyes. "I don't think Donnie Rae did it. I've known him since he was a child, and he never had a mean bone in his body."

Bertha snorted. "We are talking about killing Louie. I don't care what anyone says, Louie was mean down to his core. I think he got what he deserved."

Weenie shrugged. "I think it's sad that he's not having any kind of funeral or memorial. They are just cremating him."

Bertha took a sip of her tea. "I don't think anyone would attend a memorial. It's just as well he's being cremated. I wonder what they'll do with the ashes?"

Weenie shrugged. "Maybe they'll scatter him on the beach or on a mountain. Polly was fond of him. Plus, she has that RV. She could drive him to a pretty mountain in Colorado and scatter his ashes there."

I grimaced. "I don't think Polly has much love for Louie. I doubt she has the money or the inclination to drive his ashes to a beautiful mountain destination."

Bertha nodded. "Dove is right. Maybe they'll just flush him."

I cringed. "Down the toilet? Surely not."

Weenie shook her head. "They'll just send his urn to someplace that holds those kinds of things. For people who don't have family."

I shifted in my seat. "That's kind of sad. Even for Louie."

Weenie nodded. "Dove is right. And I'm still not convinced that Donnie Rea poisoned Louie."

Bertha looked thoughtful for a second before speaking. "Maybe he got fed up with Louie. It's no secret he was mean to everyone. I just wonder what he and Louie got in a fight about before he died."

I nodded. "Well, there's one way to find out." I finished my tea and stood. "I'm headed to the police station to see if he will talk to me."

CHAPTER 22

I pulled into the parking spot at the police department. I spotted Dean's vehicle, and I got out of my car.

When I walked in, the place was buzzing with activity. I spotted Dean on the phone looking very animated as he talked.

"Hey Dove, Dean is really busy right now and can't talk," Sloan said as he walked by.

I only nodded and started to walk back out, but something caught my eye.

The door to the hallway leading to the holding cells was open. They never left this door open.

I took a quick glance around to make sure no one was watching me, and headed through the open door and down the hallway.

The cells were all empty except for Donnie Rae sitting on the cot with his face buried in his hands.

"Donnie Rae?"

He jerked his head up at the sound of my voice. His eyes squinted. "Yes?"

I nodded and walked closer to the bars. "I know you don't know me, but I'm Dove Agnew.

He nodded. "You're Dean's girlfriend. The fancy one from New York City."

I shifted my weight. "I don't know about fancy. But yes. I used to live in New York City."

He sighed. "I used to have dreams of leaving this small town and going somewhere bigger. But then reality set in." He narrowed his eyes. "What do you want?"

I cleared my throat. "Donnie Rae, I'm here to talk to you about Louie."

His shoulders slumped, and he studied the floor. "Everyone thinks I killed him."

I blinked. "Did you?"

He looked up at me with the most sorrowful eyes I had ever seen. "No, I didn't."

I bit my lip and glanced over my shoulder making sure we were still alone. "People saw you and Louie arguing."

He nodded. "I'd caught him sneaking into Weenie's house when she wasn't home. I saw him walk out of the house and into the woods wearing a red scarf. He didn't have it on when he went in, and I knew he had stolen it. I told him that Weenie was the nicest lady in Harland Creek, and I didn't want him breaking into her house."

I smiled. "You were sticking up for her."

He nodded. "Yeah. I know what it feels like when you don't have family. Whenever I'm sick, Weenie brings me a pie. Her pies are the best. Especially her apple pie."

I studied him for a second. "What did Louie say when you told him to leave Weenie alone?"

He snorted. "Same thing he always said. He told me to mind my business before I ended up in a world of hurt. To tell you the truth, Dove, I'm surprised that Louie lived as long as he did. I heard rumors that when he was still in New York, he was working for the mob."

My eyes widened. "Really?"

He nodded.

"Dove, what are you doing back here?" Dean's voice held an urgency to it.

I spun around and smiled. "Looking for you," I lied.

He narrowed his eyes, and I knew from the look on his face he wasn't buying it.

"Say goodbye to Donnie Rae."

I smiled and gave the prisoner a little wave before hurrying out of the police station.

*a*fter the commotion, I headed back to the quilt shop. Mom was there alone.

"Slow day?" I asked.

She snorted. "Since this snowstorm came through, no one is out shopping. My customer base is old women, and they are either scared they are going to fall and break a hip, or they are out looking for Petunia."

I leaned against the cutting table. "How disappointed was Elizabeth that I didn't manage to get Petunia at the diner? I know I let her down."

Mom shook her head. "She's not mad at you. She heard how Bryson overreacted and chased her off with her raccoon friend. Bryson better hope Elizabeth Harland doesn't run into him today."

I nodded. "I can't believe he overreacted. It's like Barney Fife is now on the police force."

Mom laughed. "Well, he is from up north, dear."

I shoved off the table and looked at the book where we kept the list of quilting projects we needed to do. "I guess I should start quilting this sampler quilt."

Mom squeezed my arm. "Actually, would you mind terribly going over to Elizabeth's house and maybe reassuring her that Petunia will be found?"

I nodded. "Of course. Are you sure you don't need me here?"

She smiled. "It's slow right now. And I'd rather you be with Elizabeth. And take those blueberry muffins sitting in the basket with you. I meant to take them to her this morning but never got around to it."

I nodded. "Okay, well, don't work too much." I grabbed my purse along with the basket and headed for the door.

As I drove to Elizabeth's house, the sun was hanging low in the sky and casting a golden glow over the winter hills. Most of the snow and ice had already melted, leaving behind a muddy mess.

I turned down the winding country road and listened to the rattle of my car. I glanced over at the basket of muffins in the passenger seat. Mom made the best sourdough blueberry muffins, and the scent was making my mouth water.

I finally turned into her driveway and parked in front of the large white farmhouse. Grabbing the basket, I walked up to the front door. I spotted her face pressed up to the glass of the door before she opened it and welcomed me inside.

"Dove? Is Petunia okay?" Her worried face looked like she'd aged ten years since the goat ran off.

I smiled. "When I saw her at the diner, she seemed well-fed. She looked good to me." I glanced at the ground. "I would have had her if..." I looked up at her. "I'm sorry, Elizabeth. I let you down."

Elizabeth gave me a grateful smile. "You didn't let me down, Dove. You gave me hope."

I frowned. "I did?"

She nodded. "Yes. When Weenie and Bertha told me you saw her at the diner, I knew there was still hope." Her face darkened. "And if that new cop hadn't interfered, she would be home by now."

I sighed heavily and set the basket down on the foyer table. "I don't think he meant any harm. He's just..." I searched for the right word.

"An idiot. That's what he is." She walked past me into the kitchen. "Come have a cup of coffee."

I didn't argue.

She poured me a cup and set it in front of me at the kitchen table. She set out a saucer for the blueberry muffin. I wasted no time in tasting the delicious treat.

Elizabeth frowned as she stared at her muffin. "I'm surprised Petunia was with a raccoon. First she was spotted with some wild dogs, then behind the grocery store, after that a herd of deer on a trail camera, and now she's hanging out with a raccoon."

I chuckled. "Petunia is certainly the social butterfly. I think she likes the company and is just testing out her wings." I took a bite of the muffin and chewed thoughtfully. "You know—it's like going to college or moving to a new city, where you meet new friends."

Elizabeth cocked her head. "Dove, do you think Petunia even wants to come back? Maybe she's tired of her old life."

I brushed the crumbs off my hand. "Elizabeth, of course she wants to come back. That little goat loves you and Heather. Who knows, maybe Petunia is out there tracking down clues to who killed Louie. You know how she has helped us solve murders in the past. Maybe she is recruiting all the woodland creatures to help."

This pulled a genuine laugh out of Elizabeth. "Maybe you're right, Dove."

I smiled and finished my muffin. "Of course, I am. And just because the police have Donnie Rae in custody doesn't mean they have the right man." I leaned closer. "He admitted that he saw Louie break into Weenie's house when she wasn't home. When Louie came out, he was wearing a red scarf. Donnie Rae confronted Louie and told him to leave Weenie alone. Anyway, Dean found that same red scarf out behind Weenie's house the night she heard someone outside on her porch."

Elizabeth's eyes widened. "So how did the red scarf get out into the woods after Louie's death?"

I leaned back in my chair and sipped my coffee. "That's a great question. And I intend on finding out."

Elizabeth nodded. "Good. And I'm with you. I don't think Donnie Rae killed Louie. I do think whoever did it had a great deal of anger with him. I read a murder mystery book one time, and the killer poisoned the victim because they wanted to make them suffer. Find out who hates Louie the most, and we'll find our culprit and solve this case."

CHAPTER 24

*W*hen I left Elizabeth's home, I headed back to the Chateau RV Park. Something was pulling at me to go back and talk to Polly and Linda.

When I entered, I headed straight to Polly's RV. Her car was parked outside, so I pulled in behind her and got out.

Before I knocked on her door, the door of the RV flew open. Polly narrowed her eyes when she saw me.

"What do you want, Dove?"

I shoved my hands in my stained white coat and shrugged. "I wanted to talk."

She gave me a defeated look. "Look, I don't know anything about what happened to Louie."

I nodded. "I think you're telling me the truth, but I would like to ask you some questions, if that's okay."

Polly sighed heavily but stepped back so I could enter.

I walked inside and noted the place looked tidy. It was a big difference from the last time I had been there.

"Want some coffee?" she asked.

"No thanks. I just had some at Elizabeth Harland's house." I sat on the couch. "Look, Polly. As much as Louie broke your heart, I don't think you would have killed him. I think you were more heartbroken than vengeful. And it would be helpful if you had an alibi for the time he was killed."

Polly sat across from me, and her shoulders slumped. "I went to Jackson early on the morning of the snowstorm to meet someone. Because of the snow, I couldn't get back, so I had to get a hotel for the night."

I leaned forward. "Okay, so who were you with?"

She looked at the floor. "I went to a bookstore and talked to the owner. I wanted to see if he would be interested in having me do a book signing with my new book that I am working on."

I smiled. "That's exciting."

She looked up at me. "Not really. He said he only has book signings for popular authors. I left there feeling like a loser. Again."

I felt bad for Polly. "I'm sorry that happened, Polly. I think once this new book of yours comes out, it will be a game changer and things will look up."

She gave me a hapless look. "You think so, Dove? Because I don't. I'm tired. Tired of being in survival mode. I'm tired of no one ever choosing me. My husband chose his lover. Louie chose my money over me. Do you know what that feels like? To always feel like a loser? What's the point of even trying?"

From the slump of her shoulders to the defeated look in her eyes, I could see Polly felt like a failure.

I swallowed hard. "I know a lot about feeling like a loser."

She looked at me as if she didn't believe me.

"I had a successful design business in New York. I had a fabulous penthouse, made a name for myself, and had a French boyfriend. And then my partner committed a crime, and my business was suddenly gone. I had to move home to live with my mom and start my life all over again, from scratch."

Her eyes widened with each word of my story. "Really? I had no idea, Dove."

I shrugged. "Well, it's true. And for what it's worth, I don't think you are a loser. I think you are a survivor. You just must keep going."

She gave me a ghost of a smile.

"I think you need to tell Dean all this. He needs to know where you were on the day Louie died so he can eliminate you as a suspect."

She nodded. "I'll call him." Polly frowned. "You said you just came from Elizabeth Harland's house. I heard about her little goat. I hope she finds her."

I nodded. "We have had sightings of her with some dogs, then a herd of deer, and then I saw her myself in the kitchen of the diner, but then she ran off. She had a raccoon with her."

Polly's eyes lit up. "She was with a herd of deer and a raccoon."

I nodded "She sure was."

Excitement shone on the woman's face. "Maybe Petunia thinks she is a donkey."

I frowned. "What are you talking about?"

Polly stood and grabbed her notebook and pen off the table and sat back down.

"I've heard of donkeys running off and joining herds of different species, and they fit right in. You see, donkeys are very protective. And it seems like the deer—and you said a raccoon? —have taken Petunia in as one of their own. She might not be an actual donkey, but she is very protective, and maybe they know that and have adopted her."

I sat back and grinned. "Maybe they have. I mean, she is protective with those she is close to. She's gotten me out of a jam a time or two. And she's smart."

Polly jotted something down in the notebook. "This has

given me an idea for a book." She looked up at me. "Do you mind if I write this down?"

I smiled. "Of course not. I think it's great that Petunia has given you some inspiration."

Polly looked at me and gave me a genuine smile. "I think Petunia just might have saved my writing career."

I stood. "That's a lovely thing to say, Polly. I'll leave you so you can write." I reached for the door. "And I want you let me know when this book comes out."

Polly's face brightened as she tapped the pen to her lip. "Don't worry, Dove. If this book comes out like I think it might, my first book signing will be in Harland Creek."

I smiled as I walked to my car. We might not have found Petunia, but it certainly sounded like Polly had found herself.

CHAPTER 25

s soon as I stepped out of Polly's RV, I headed toward Linda's camper. I froze when I saw her coming out the door. I quickly ducked behind a tree to see what she was up to.

She glanced around as if making sure no one was watching her and then slid a large backpack on her back and headed out into the woods.

I pulled out my phone and sent a quick text to Dean telling him I was at the Chateau RV Park. I hesitated before sending a second text telling him I was following Linda Martinez through the woods.

I knew Dean would be mad, but figured I needed him to know where I was in case, I went missing.

I shoved my hands into my pockets and headed into the woods.

Linda was probably in her mid-fifties, and I was surprised how fast she was walking through the woods and the brambles. I struggled to keep up with her.

Linda suddenly stopped. I quickly ducked behind a tree. I held my breath, hoping she didn't spot me.

I heard the snap of a branch, and my heart sank. Had she found me?

"Linda, what took you so long?" A male's voice split the silence of the forest.

I relaxed when I figured out I had not been discovered.

Carefully and quietly, I peeked out from the cover of the large tree. It was Skipper Johnson!

"Skipper, it takes time to get the stuff you need together." Linda scoffed. "You should be grateful that I'm even making the effort."

Skipper reached inside his camo jacket and pulled out a package of beef jerky and waved it in the air. "Do you know how tired I am of eating this stuff? I hope you packed some canned goods inside that backpack."

Linda threw the backpack on the ground and glared. "You ungrateful brat. You should be thanking me that I packed a sleeping bag and a tent. It will be better than that lean-to you've been sleeping under."

His eyes lit up when she mentioned a proper tent. "What about water?"

She narrowed her eyes. "I couldn't fit it in. I put a filtration straw in there. You should be able to drink from any ponds or bodies of water with it."

He nodded and knelt beside the backpack. He unzipped the top and began to rifle through the items inside.

"Are the cops even asking about me?" he asked as he examined a can of beans.

"No. In fact, they have arrested Donnie Rae."

Skipper looked up in surprise. "Donnie Rae?"

Linda nodded. "They know that Donnie Rae and Louie argued before his death. And then Donnie Rae tried to skip town before the police could question him."

He blinked and stood up. "Think I can go home now?"

Linda hissed. "No, your idiot You can't go anywhere until

Donnie Rae is formally charged with Louie's death. Right now, they are charging him for taking a hostage."

Skipper stood up and stared at Linda. "Taking a hostage? Who did he take?"

Linda snorted. "He tried to take Mrs. Simpson at Mac's Grocery. But when he came out with her in the wheelchair, she started beating the crap out of him with her umbrella."

Skipper looked thoughtful. "Mrs. Simpson was always mean. I had her in second grade. She threatened to spank me because I didn't read ten books in a week." He shrugged. "So how much longer do I have to stay hidden, Linda?"

I eased back behind the tree and continued to listen.

"You'll stay hidden until I come get you. You are still spending the night by that old, abandoned house, right?"

He nodded. "Yeah, but I get scared at night. I think that old house is haunted. Last night I kept hearing strange sounds, like bleating or something."

Linda laughed. "You are probably hearing that lost goat, Petunia. Everyone in town is looking for her. Dove almost had her at the diner, but she let her get away."

I gritted my teeth together. I most certainly did not let Petunia get away. That was all on Bryson's shoulders.

"Anyway, just stay hidden for a few more days, and don't build any fires."

Skipper groaned. "But it's cold at night."

Linda growled. "I don't care. People will see the smoke from the fire and come investigate. Then the cops will grab you. You're the one with a criminal record. You just can't chance it. Besides, the sleeping bag will keep you warm."

Silence stretched between them.

"Thanks, Linda," Skipper finally said.

Linda sighed heavily. "We must look out for one another. Just stick to the plan and everything will work out, okay?"

I heard the rustle of leaves as Skipper gathered his items

and put them back into his backpack. Linda started walking back to the RV park.

I eased around the tree until neither could see me as they walked away. I waited until I was sure neither Skipper nor Linda could see me and then began to walk back out of the woods. When I finally broke through the tree line and into the RV park, I looked around for Linda. When I didn't see her, I made a run for my car and started the engine.

I drove as fast as I could to the police station.

CHAPTER 26

I ran into the police station and glanced around for Dean. I went to his office and found it empty.

"Hey Dove, are you looking for Dean?" Sloan stopped at the door of Dean's office.

"Yeah, I need to talk to him," I said breathlessly.

"Sorry, he said he had to go to the Chateau RV Park. Said it was an emergency."

I sighed. "Dang. That emergency was me." I pulled out my cell phone and sent him a text.

Sloan frowned. "Is everything okay?"

I nodded. "Yes, but there is something you need to know. I know where Skipper Johnson is."

"So?"

I narrowed my eyes. "Skipper worked full time for Farmer Brown. He had access to the poison that killed Louie. Not to mention he has a record."

Sloan crossed his arms over his chest. "What's Skipper's motive for killing Louie?"

I blinked and went quiet. "I don't know. But I know that Linda is helping Skipper hide in the woods near the RV park.

I heard her say they need to look out for each other and stick to the plan

Sloan's eyes widened. "What did she mean by that?"

I huffed. "If I knew that, I wouldn't be here asking for help solving this crime. I bit my lip. "I should be telling Dean this."

Sloan parked his hands on his hips. "Well, you're just going to have to tell me. Now start from the beginning."

I nodded. "I followed Linda Martinez into the woods behind the RV park. She met up with Skipper and gave him a backpack full of camping supplies and canned goods."

Sloan's eyes widened. "Linda is helping Skipper." Then he frowned. "We have Donnie Rae in custody. He is the most likely suspect."

I cocked my head. "What if you have the wrong guy? I mean, did Donnie Rae admit to anything?"

Sloan narrowed his eyes on me. "You know I can't tell you anything about this case."

I shook my head. "Fine. Well, at least go after Dean and make sure he has some backup."

Sloan glared at me. I knew he didn't like taking my advice.

"If you don't go help him, I will." I lifted my chin.

"Don't you dare." Sloan pointed a finger at me. "You stay here, and I'll take some backup with me."

I walked around the desk and sat in Dean's chair. "Tell Dean to call me when you find him. I need to know he's okay."

Sloan nodded and pulled the door closed.

I watched through the blinds as five cars pulled out of the police station and headed in the direction of the Chateau RV Park.

CHAPTER 27

I sat in Dean's office and continued to stare at my phone, waiting for an answer from Dean.

Bryson popped his head in the office and smiled. He had a glazed donut in his hand. "Hi, Dove. Are you waiting for Dean?"

I nodded and stared at the sugary treat. "Yeah. He's out, but I'm hoping he'll be back before long."

Bryson followed my gaze. "You want a donut? There's some left in the breakroom. But I would hurry before everyone eats them all."

I jumped up from my seat. "Thanks." I made my way to the breakroom. When I entered, the scent of coffee and sugar wrapped around me like a big hug. I opened the donut box, snagged a glistening glazed donut, and took a bite before heading to the coffeepot.

"We really need a Keurig," Mitch said as he walked over to the donuts. He eyed the donut I had in my hand and smiled. "Feeding your addiction, I see."

Everyone in town knew donuts were my weakness. I didn't care.

"I could have a worse addiction."

Mitch snorted. "That's true."

I chewed thoughtfully. "You didn't go with Dean to check out the Chateau RV Park?"

His eyes widened. "Oh, I was there. It seemed like when we showed up Linda tipped off Skipper. Dean called in the state police to help since we don't have the manpower for that."

I frowned. "And you came back?"

Mitch snorted. "Yeah. He didn't want the safety of the town of Harland Creek to be at the mercy of Bryson."

I nodded slowly. "He seems nice enough."

Mitch's eyes hardened. "Nice won't cut it in law enforcement. He's soft. A little too soft." Mitch sighed. "Anyway, so I'm back here manning the station."

I finished off my donut and decided against a cup of coffee. "In that case, I should be on my way. I need to be looking for Petunia."

Mitch nodded. "You would have had her, too, if Bryson didn't mess things up."

I cringed. "I know. I kind of feel bad for him, you know?"

Mitch snorted. "Yeah. He's been getting some crappy jobs. Farmer Brown thought his prize pig went missing and called us. We sent Bryson. Turns out it had wandered into Agnes Jackson's land and turned over one of her beehives. She's thinking of suing the pig."

I let out a laugh. "I didn't hear about that. I guess everyone has been so focused on finding Petunia."

Mitch took a sip of his coffee as his radio buzzed. "I've got to get this." He headed out of the breakroom.

I brushed off my hands and decided to head on back to the quilt shop. Maybe Mom had heard some news about Petunia.

On my way out the door, Bryson gave me a friendly wave.

I waved back, feeling a little bad we had been talking about him.

I climbed in my car and grimaced when I looked down at my coat. I had not had time to get it cleaned. I was beginning to think it was ruined.

I turned my car in the direction of the cleaners. Traffic was sparse, as the townsfolk of Harland Creek didn't dare venture out in the cold weather. I smiled, remembering my winters spent in New York City.

The city did indeed not sleep. Where winter drove people indoors in Harland Creek, winter coaxed people out to see the wonders of ice skating and Christmas trees and venues lit up like a magical kingdom.

I pulled into an empty parking spot at the Harland Creek Cleaners and hurried out of the car.

When I stepped inside, Mr. Wilson, the owner, looked up from his newspaper and smiled. "Dove! I'm surprised to see you here."

I smiled at the older man with the handlebar mustache.

"I dropped by to see if this could be saved." I spread my arms out and looked down at my mud-stained, once white coat.

His eyebrows shot up, and he scratched his chin. "It may be a challenge, but I just may be able to save it. Can you give me a couple of days to work on it?"

I brightened at his words. "I'll give you a week if you think you can bring it back to life." I slid the wool coat off and handed it to him.

He frowned when he saw I was only wearing a thin long-sleeved t-shirt under the coat.

"You have another coat to wear?"

I bit my lip. "Not on me, but I bet I can scrounge some-thing up in Mom's closet."

He shook his head and headed to a rack of cleaned

clothes. "Your mother would wring my neck if she saw I let you go out in the weather like that. I have a coat here that no one ever picked up. I've left messages with the owner, but it's been two months now." He pulled the plastic off the brown-looking coat. "It's not fancy like your coat, but it will keep you warm." He handed it to me.

It was a brown barn coat that was lined with fleece. "Thank you." I slipped the coat on. The sleeves were too long and went past my hands, but it was incredibly warm. "I really appreciate it."

Mr. Wilson smiled. "Glad to help." He picked up my coat and pointed to the back room. "I'll get started on this today and will give you a call when it's done."

I nodded as I snuggled down into my borrowed coat. "Thanks, Mr. Wilson. I appreciate it."

Stepping outside, I was grateful for my brown coat. It might not look as fashionable, but at least I was warm.

CHAPTER 28

*T*he quilting ladies had gathered at the quilt shop when I got back. I was surprised to see even Elizabeth was there.

I frowned when I saw all the quilting ladies gathered around Mom's computer. "What's going on?"

Weenie looked at me. "Your mom is watching Facebook Live. Looks like Dean and the state police have Skipper surrounded. They are trying to get him to come out on his own before they send Tarzan in."

I leaned over Weenie's shoulder to see the screen. "Who is filming this?"

Agnes laughed. "Farmer Brown. They called him in to try to talk Skipper into coming out on his own. Skipper refused, saying he was innocent, and they were trying to pin Louie's murder on him because of his record. Skipper said he was trying to leave town because he had gotten his life together and wanted to be able to see his daughter again. It seems like when he was in prison, his ex-wife refused to let him contact his daughter."

I blinked. "That's sad. But doesn't he know that the cops have Donnie Rae in custody?"

Mom looked up at me. "Yes, but he doesn't trust the cops."

Agnes cut her eyes at me. "Maybe because Skipper knows that Donnie Rae is not the one who murdered Louie."

Maggie spoke up. "The poison that killed Louie is an insecticide that Farmer Brown kept on his farm. The insecticide was banned, and Farmer Brown is adamant that he hadn't used it in a while."

Agnes narrowed her eyes. "I bet Farmer Brown killed Louie."

Everyone snorted. "Agnes, Farmer Brown couldn't hurt a fly. You're only saying that because you two have an ongoing feud about something—what, no one knows," Elizabeth stated. "You need to get over it."

Agnes glared but didn't say anything.

"Skipper has motive, and he had access to the poison. We should give him a name." I stated.

Weenie's eyebrows shot up behind her glasses. "How about Courthouse Steps?"

I grinned. "That's pretty good, Weenie. That's a perfect name."

Elizabeth frowned. "Polly has already been eliminated. But I don't know what connection Linda has to Skipper. Do you think if Skipper did poison Louie, Linda was in on it?"

Sylvia spoke up this time. "Honestly? I don't think so. I think Linda doesn't have many friends, and she took Skipper under her wing. They were both kind of outcasts. She doesn't trust people either."

My heart twisted a little. "That's so sad."

Maggie nodded. "It is. And Linda didn't have it in her to kill Louie. She may look all mean and tough, but it's a façade. One day as she was getting ready to leave the saloon, Eleanor made a comment on Linda's old clothes. I could see that it hurt her feelings, but Linda looked at me and said she's used to it. People have made fun of her since she was a little girl."

Sylvia nodded. "I remember that. I made sure to slip some laxative into Eleanor's coffee as she was getting her hair done. And then I locked our bathroom door due to it being out of service." She arched her eyebrows. "You should have seen her struggle to make it to the bathroom at the donut shop. Funniest day ever."

Chortles went up around the room.

"We are back to Donnie Rae or Skipper being the killer." I shook my head. "I just don't think he could do it." I looked at Weenie.

"Weenie, I went to see Donnie Rae. He told me he followed Louie to your house one day. He saw him use the code to get into your house and when he came out, he was wearing a red scarf."

Weenie's eyes widened. "He saw him?"

I nodded. "He said he followed Louie because he knew he was up to no good and didn't want him to hurt you. Donnie Rae said he threatened Louie that if he ever came back to your house, he would have to deal with him." I gave her a slight smile. "Donnie Rae told me you were the nicest woman he has ever met, and he didn't want Louie doing anything to hurt you."

Weenie's eyes warmed at the compliment. "Donnie Rae was always a sweet boy."

Bertha grunted. "Well, we can't have both Donnie Rae and Skipper innocent. One of them killed Louie. Unless y'all think Weenie did it."

Weenie blinked.

I snorted. "Nobody thinks Weenie killed Louie. That's ludicrous."

Weenie lifted her chin. "I guess everyone thinks I'm weak. That I couldn't defend myself."

The room went silent.

I cleared my throat. "Weenie, what do you mean that you couldn't defend yourself? Did Louie do something to you?"

Weenie sniffed. "I've lived on my own all my life. I may be small, but I'm not a pushover."

Bertha sighed heavily. "No one thinks you're a pushover, Weenie."

I cocked my head. "Weenie, you never told me how you got the bruises on your arm."

Elizabeth's eyes widened. "What bruises?"

Weenie pressed her lips together.

I looked at Elizabeth. "The day Louie was found dead, Weenie had bruises on her arm in the shape of fingerprints. Louie did it."

Bertha glared at Weenie. "Why didn't you tell me?"

Weenie shrugged. "Because I was afraid you would go off the deep end, Bertha. You have anger issues. You should try anger management classes."

Bertha gave her friend an offended look. "I'm not angry. I'm a perfectly content person. I just can't stand idiots."

Agnes shook her head. "Let's get back to Weenie's bruises." She reached over and squeezed Weenie's hand. "Honey, when did Louie grab you?"

Weenie shook her head. "It wasn't Louie that grabbed me."

I blinked. "It wasn't? Then who was it?"

Weenie shrugged her shoulders. "It was Donnie Rae."

An audible gasp went up around the room.

"So Donnie Rae is the killer." Sylvia breathed out.

Weenie shook her head. "No, he's not. Donnie Rae didn't mean to hurt me."

I cocked my head. "Then explain what you mean."

Weenie took a deep breath and clasped her hands together. "The day before the snowstorm, I was walking out to my car. Donnie Rae pulled up. He said he wanted to warn me that Louie had been hanging around my house. He said he knew in the past that Louie had broken into my home and eaten my pie. I put a lot of love in my pies and Louie was the last person on earth who deserved something I made. I wasn't going to put up with it anymore." Weenie looked at me. "That's why I had that knife in my hand when you saw me standing over Louie. I always kept a knife with me. Just in case."

Elizabeth walked over and pulled Weenie into a hug. "Oh, Weenie. I'm so sorry you didn't feel safe in your own home. What a horrible way to live."

Weenie smiled and patted Elizabeth on the cheek. "I'm tougher than I look."

Elizabeth smiled. "Yes, you are."

I caught Weenie's gaze. "So how did Donnie Rae leave bruises on you?"

She gave me a sheepish look. "I thanked Donnie Rae for letting me know. I was headed to my car, and my foot slipped. Donnie Rae grabbed me, preventing me from falling. He left bruises. That's all."

I nodded slowly. "That makes sense."

Bertha looked at me. "Donnie Rae had a motive for killing Louie. But what about Skipper? This case has me stumped."

I nodded and turned to look out the window. "Yeah, I know. I want to talk to Skipper, but that seems to be impossible."

Mom stood from her computer. "Talk to the person closest to Skipper."

I spun around and looked at her. "Who would that be?"

Mom gave me a grin. "His boss. Farmer Brown."

CHAPTER 29

I pulled behind the group of police cars that were near the woods. I slipped out of my car and spotted Sloan yelling at Farmer Brown for broadcasting the situation live on Facebook.

Farmer Brown looked down at the ground and seemed quite ashamed of himself.

I felt bad for the man. I headed in that direction, and Sloan narrowed his eyes on me.

"Dove, what are you doing here?"

I shrugged. "I'm here to see if I can do anything." I looked at Farmer Brown. "Are you okay?"

Sloan interrupted. "He's going to be in a lot of trouble for putting this stuff on Facebook. This is an ongoing situation."

I put my arm around Farmer Brown. "Why don't we go over there, out of the way?"

Farmer Brown gave me a grateful smile. As we walked away, Sloan called out. "Keep him out of trouble."

I nodded and walked Farmer Brown over to the back of his truck. I let the tailgate down, and we both sat.

"I was just trying to help. I feel bad for Skipper. He's

trying to turn his life around, and I'm afraid they'll try to pin this on him."

I nodded. "Because of his criminal past?"

Farmer Brown sighed heavily. "Yes. Skipper is the best worker I have ever had. I know he had a bad history, but I wanted to give him a second chance. He goes beyond what I ask him to do. Dove, he didn't kill Louie."

I nodded. "Tell me about the day he ran off."

Farmer Brown took a deep breath. "Skipper got scared when the cops showed up again."

I held up my hand. "The first time was when your pig went missing."

He nodded. "Someone kidnapped my prize pig. I told Dean to send someone out pronto." He glared. "Instead of sending someone capable like Sloan or Mitch, he sends that Yankee out here." He shook his head.

"Are you talking about Bryson?"

He nodded. "Yes. That fool acted like it wasn't a big deal that my pig was gone. He told me that the pig probably ran off." He snorted. "Can you imagine an animal just running off?"

I sighed heavily. "That's what happened to Petunia."

Farmer Brown shook his head furiously. "I don't think Petunia ran off. I think she was kidnapped, just like my pig."

I frowned. "But you got your pig back."

He gave me a sheepish look. "She was found at one of Agnes's beehives."

I nodded, trying to follow the story. "So was Skipper nervous when the cops came out the first time?"

Farmer Brown swiped his brow. "He is always nervous when he sees the police. He has some PTSD from being in prison and doesn't like to be around the cops. Not to mention what Louie tried to pull." He looked over at me.

I immediately perked up. "What did Louie do?"

Farmer Brown blew out a breath. "I promised Skipper I would not say anything…"

I reached over and squeezed his hand. "You need to come clean so the situation doesn't get any worse."

He nodded. "Louie knew about Skipper's past. He came to Skipper and wanted him to sell drugs for him in Jackson. Skipper flat out refused. Louie said he was either going to sell drugs for him one way or the other."

I frowned. "What did that mean?"

Farmer Brown scowled. "Louie planted drugs in Skipper's truck. When the cops showed up the first time regarding my pig, Skipper freaked out and thought Louie had called the cops on him and was trying to frame him."

My mouth dropped. "Did Skipper go to the cops and tell them what happened?"

Farmer Brown gave me a look like I had grown a second head. "Are you serious? Skipper knew the cops wouldn't believe him. He's been trying to turn his life around so he can get visitation rights to see his daughter. Going to the cops would just make things worse. Instead, Skipper flushed the drugs and stayed away from Louie. I guess I need to tell Dean, so he'll understand Skipper's reason for hiding. I was only filming so nothing would happen to Skipper when he came out. The man is scared to death."

I eased off the tailgate. "Thanks for clearing that up, Farmer Brown." I looked back over at the tree line, where cops were going in and out of the forest. "Are you going to go home?"

He shook his head. "No. I'm going to stay until Skipper comes out. I want him to know at least someone believes him."

I gave him a smile. As I walked back to my car, I reflected on the old man's words.

And I was more convinced than ever that Skipper was not Louie's killer.

I felt like the killer was so close, yet so far away.

Once I got into my car, I headed back to Weenie's house to see if I had missed something at the scene of the crime.

CHAPTER 30

When I pulled up to Weenie's house, her car wasn't there. I killed the engine and got out of the car.

I was back at the scene of the crime.

Standing there for a second, I closed my eyes and inhaled the sting of the cold air. The distinct sound of a cardinal and the chattering of a gray squirrel made me realize how isolated Weenie was out here in the country.

I glanced toward the tree that Donnie Rae had spied Louie walking out of when he broke into Weenie's house. He left the same way and probably got his scarf so tangled up in the briar and thorns that he left it behind. That would explain how Dean found it in the woods.

I thought back to the night Dean had found it and brought it inside Weenie's house to me.

I wondered why Louie would take something so insignificant as a scarf. But then I knew. Louie was mean. He could take something he thought would mean something to Weenie. Her prized possessions of her mother tucked safely away in the trunk in the attic was like hitting the jackpot to Louie.

He took whatever meant something to someone else. I remembered the phrase "mean for sport." That described Louie to a T. He had a black heart that would never be redeemed.

I heard something from the back of the house and tensed up.

Quietly, I crept around to the back of the house. I frowned when I spotted Bryson bent down at the back door.

"Bryson?"

He jumped up and spun around. When he saw me, he smiled. "Dove. I didn't hear you walk up."

I relaxed. "Didn't mean to startle you." I glanced up at the house. "I'm guessing Weenie isn't home."

He shook his head. "No. Last I heard, there was a sighting of Petunia near Agnes Jackson's house. I heard from Mitch all the quilters were headed over there to hopefully catch her."

My eyebrows shot up. "Really? That's great." I nodded toward the back door. "What are you doing here?"

He sighed heavily and parked his hands on his hips. "I wanted to come back and have another look at the crime scene." He gave me a sincere look. "You know, Dove, I don't believe Donnie Rae is the killer."

I walked over the back steps and leaned against the railing to look up at him. "Does anyone else share your feeling?"

Bryson's brow creased in worry. "No. And I don't want someone who is innocent going to jail. That's why I wanted to have another look here at the crime scene."

My heart softened at his words. "I'm glad to hear you say that Bryson. I don't think Donnie Rae is guilty, either. But unfortunately, he's the one locked up now."

Bryson sighed heavily. "I'm going to sweep the area around the house to make sure we didn't miss anything."

I nodded. "Mind if I look at the porch?"

He waved me forward. "Be my guest. But let me know if you find anything."

I chortled. "You're unlike Sloan. He doesn't much like it when I try to help."

Bryson grinned. "I welcome the help. We need to do whatever it takes to make this world safe." He strode off toward the tree line.

I climbed the steps onto the porch and glanced around. I didn't see anything, so I pressed my face to the glass of the door and looked inside.

The lights were off, but I could still make out the shadows and outlines of furniture, like the kitchen table and chairs. I glanced over to the kitchen island where Louie's body had been discovered.

Nothing seemed off.

Bryson came running out of the woods, holding up an item that looked like leather. "Dove! Look!"

I hurried toward him. "Did you find something?"

I stopped in front of him and saw he was holding up a pair of leather work gloves.

"It's a pair of work gloves that belong to Skipper," he said proudly.

"How do you know?"

He snickered. "Because when I went over to Farmer Brown's farm the first time, I saw Skipper wearing these same gloves." He looked at them. "And I bet if we test the inside, Skipper's DNA will be on the inside and the poison that killed Louie will be on the outside. He must have left them behind after he poisoned Louie."

I frowned. "Shouldn't you put that into some kind of plastic bag? You know, to preserve the evidence?"

His eyebrows shot up. "You're right." He reached into the inside pocket of his police jacket, pulled out a plastic bag, and put the gloves on the inside. "Thanks for the reminder."

Bryson gave my arm a squeeze. "I need to get this back to the station. Are you okay out here by yourself?"

I nodded. "Sure. I'm about to leave as well."

As I watched Bryson pull out of Weenie's driveway, I couldn't help but feel sad that the killer was Skipper.

CHAPTER 31

couldn't sleep that night. After I got home, Dean had called and informed me that Skipper had finally been captured. While he continued to plead his innocence, the evidence was overwhelming. Farmer Brown verified that the gloves Bryson found were indeed Skipper's.

Donnie Rae was also still behind bars due to holding Mrs. Simpson hostage.

And Petunia was still missing. The sighting at Agnes's house had been a hoax that someone called in.

After tossing and turning, I finally got out of bed and crept downstairs. Glancing at the time on the microwave, I noted it was three a.m.

There was no way I could go back to sleep, so I decided to make some coffee. I started the coffeepot, grabbed my laptop at the kitchen table, and waited for the coffee to be ready.

I scrolled through mindless social media until the coffee brewed. I shut the laptop, grabbed a cup of coffee, and headed into the living room. Grabbing a quilt off the back of the sofa, I wrapped up in it and let my mind wander.

Things just didn't make sense to me. Why would Skipper

kill Louie? Half the town hated Louie and had more motivation to kill him than Skipper.

I sipped my coffee and wished I could get answers to my questions. Maybe Sloan was right. Maybe I had no business getting involved in solving this crime.

Out of the quiet, I heard a bump at the front door. I froze in place, unable to move.

Maybe I was imagining things. I was sleep-deprived, after all.

Suddenly there was another bump at the door. I jumped.

Sitting my coffee down on the coffee table, I looked around for some kind of weapon. There was nothing but magazines and a sewing basket. My eyes darted around until I spotted the fireplace poker.

I took a steadying breath and reached for the poker. With my heart thudding in my chest, I crept to the front door.

I tried looking out the window but couldn't see anything. Bracing myself, I grabbed the doorknob and turned.

I threw the door open. I gasped at who was standing on the other side.

Standing at the door was Petunia. There were leaves in her fur and some dried vines tangled in her horns. She had lost some weight but didn't seem harmed.

I dropped the poker, and my knees buckled. I fell to the floor and started sobbing.

Petunia let out a bleat and walked inside. She nuzzled me with her head, her horns getting tangled in my hair. I laughed and gently pushed her away. Sitting back on my knees, I held my arms open. "Petunia. I've missed you."

She stepped into my arms like a toddler giving a hug. She didn't let me hug her very long. Petunia bleated and walked toward the kitchen. She looked back at me and bleated impatiently.

"I know, I know. You're hungry." I got off the floor and

shut the door before hurrying into the kitchen. I flung open the refrigerator and pulled out some leftover lasagna that we had eaten the day before.

I put some on a paper plate and heated it up.

While my back was turned, Petunia put her head in the casserole dish and began eating the pasta cold.

"Hey, stop that. You'll get an upset tummy." I brushed her away before putting the casserole dish away.

She headbutted me in the back hard enough that I lost my balance and fell to the floor on my stomach. Suddenly her hot breath was on my neck.

I gasped.

"Petunia, that wasn't a demon who knocked me down on Weenie's porch. It was you!"

I got to my knees, and she let out another bleat.

Laughing, I stood up.

I tested the temperature of the lasagna before putting it on the floor. She gobbled it up and then looked up at me with sauce on her lips.

I spotted a covered dish of sugar cookies on the kitchen counter and picked up five. I hand-fed her each cookie as I stroked her head. "I'm glad you are okay, Petunia. We should call Elizabeth." I looked over at the time. "It's not even four o'clock yet. We'll wait until six o'clock and call her, okay?"

Petunia let out a bleat and walked into the living room. She looked at me and then jumped on the couch and curled up.

Laughing, I lay on the other end of the couch, covering both of us up with a quilt.

"The case might not be solved like I wanted, but at least you are home, Petunia."

CHAPTER 32

*T*he next morning, I woke up with all the quilting ladies staring down at me.

Blinking I sat up. "What?"

Elizabeth had covered her mouth with her hands. "Petunia. She's here."

I nodded. "Sorry I didn't call, but she got here around four o'clock, and I didn't want to wake you up."

Bertha gasped. "Petunia found her way all the way here?"

I nodded.

"Petunia has traveled all over the county. First hanging with some dogs, then a herd of deer, then befriending a raccoon, and now she's in town." Weenie blinked.

"She's quite the traveler. See, I told you we need to take her on more road trips." Agnes laughed. "I was sure that she would be found at my beehive when we got the call from Bryson."

I stretched and then froze. "Bryson called you. I thought Mitch called you."

Agnes shook her head. "No, it was Bryson. He was very insistent that Petunia was spotted at my beehives."

Wheels in my head started turning. I threw off the quilts, raced to the kitchen, and opened my laptop.

"What's going on, Dove?" Mom asked. All the other ladies followed me into the kitchen.

My fingers flew over the keyboard as I typed in Bryson Nicolas's name. I continued to search until I found what I was looking for.

I looked up at everyone. "We need to get to Skipper now before it's too late."

CHAPTER 33

*H*alf the quilting ladies were piled into my car, while the other half piled in Maggie's car.

"Slow down, Dove! You're coming into the parking lot on two wheels," Bertha growled.

"Hang on, then," I shot back. "I've ridden with you enough times to know you aren't the safest driver."

Bertha started to say something, but I hit a patch of black ice and skidded into the parking lot. Luckily, I landed in a parking spot beside a patrol car.

"Wow, Dove. You should drive for NASCAR," Weenie stated from the backseat. Petunia let out a bleat in agreement.

I flung open the door and darted inside.

Dean was standing at the front desk, talking to Sloan.

He frowned. "Dove?" He glanced over my shoulder. "What is everyone doing here?"

I pressed my hands against his chest. "Dean, I know who killed Louie."

He gave a grave smile. "I know, Dove. Skipper did."

I shook my head as the quilting ladies filed in behind me. "Dean, you need to listen to Dove!" Maggie shouted.

He looked down at me.

"It wasn't Skipper." I glanced around the station. "Where is Bryson?"

Dean shrugged. "He went to take Skipper his meal in the holding cell."

My eyes widened. "By himself?"

Dean nodded. "Yeah, why?"

I felt the blood drain from my face. "Bryson killed Louie. Check out his background. Look and see who his father was and who killed him. But if you don't get back to that cell right now, Skipper is going to end up dead."

Dean gave me a quizzical look but glanced at Sloan. "Tell Lenora to pull up everything we have on Bryson." Dean hurried back to the holding cell.

Sloan and I raced down the hallway behind him. Dean stopped short and froze.

"Where's Skipper?" Dean looked back at Sloan.

Sloan pointed to the back door. "They must have gone out the back door."

Dean pulled out his gun and carefully went through the back door.

Sloan looked at me and frowned. "Stay here." I watched him disappear through the door.

Curling my hands into fists, I knew I couldn't just stay here and do nothing. Ignoring Sloan's command, I went back to the entrance of the police station. I knew if Bryson was trying to make a break for it, he would have to drive past where we had parked to get onto the street.

"What's going on, Dove?" Bertha asked as I raced to the front door.

"Bryson left with Skipper out the back door." I called over my shoulder.

The cold air hit my face as I headed outside. I heard heavy panting at my side and realized that Tarzan had followed me.

I came to a stop when I reached the back of the police building. I glanced at Tarzan and commanded him to sit while I stepped into sight.

Skipper's hands were cuffed behind his back. Bryson was standing behind him with one hand on his shoulder and the other resting on his gun. Skipper's eyes were drifting shut, and he was having problems standing up.

Dean had his hands out as if he were trying to calm a horse. "What are you doing, Bryson? Skipper isn't scheduled to leave the jail," Dean stated calmly.

Bryson gave an easy smile. "It's okay, Dean. Skipper said he was having some chest pain. I thought it best that I take him down to the ER since we don't have a nurse on call at the police department."

Dean narrowed his eyes.

I held my breath.

"No, that's not how we follow procedure here, Bryson. Just bring Skipper back in."

Bryson laughed. "It's okay. We'll be back in a second, Dean." He took a step to the car.

"I said no," Dean barked back.

Bryson's calm demeanor darkened, and he drew his gun. "I don't think you understand, Dean."

I cleared my throat and took a step forward. "I do, Bryson."

Bryson turned his attention to me, clearly shocked to see me standing there at the corner of the building. "Dove."

I held my hands up to show him I had no weapon. "I know what happened, Bryson."

He looked at me as if he thought I were lying.

I lowered my hands. "I know that your father was a police officer in New York. He was a good man."

Bryson lifted his chin. "He was the best man that ever lived."

I nodded in agreement. "I know he was working on a case involving the mafia. And that they sent someone to kill your dad. That person was Louie. Louie killed your dad, didn't he, Bryson?"

Grief swept across Bryson's face. "There were a lot of dirty cops on the force. My dad wasn't one of them. My dad was shot in front of our house as we were playing baseball in the front yard. Do you know how awful it is to see your father gunned down?" Bryson's face darkened. "And the shooter didn't even hide his face from me. When he drove by, do you know what he did?"

I shook my head. "No, what?"

Bryson glared. "He smiled. Louie's face was etched in my head. I had never forgotten what he looked like. I vowed that day to avenge my father's death and make the killer pay. I was patient and eventually went to the police academy. Once I was hired on at the police department, I constantly researched Louie and everything about his life. I learned he had moved to Harland Creek and decided to try to get trans-ferred here. It's amazing how easy it is to act inept if you really try. Anyway, I followed Louie here to make him pay for what he did to my dad. Except Louie's death wasn't that quick."

I noticed that Dean and Sloan were easing closer to Bryson. Bryson noticed the motion and aimed his gun toward them. They stopped moving.

"Tell me how Louie ended up dying, Bryson."

A cruel grin stretched across his face. "It's amazing the things you can find on a farm. When I got the call to go out to Farmer Brown's farm about his missing pig, I was irritated at first. But then I saw that pesticide. I took some with me in an evidence vial when the old man wasn't looking. And after discovering that Skipper was an ex-con, it made sense to kill two birds with one stone."

I gasped. "But Skipper is innocent. He didn't kill Louie. You framed him."

Bryson growled. "He's not innocent. Do you know what he went to jail for? Hit and run while driving under the influence of drugs. He killed a man. He killed Donnie Rae's father. I know how that feels."

My eyes widened. "He served his time. And he has turned his life around."

I studied Bryson. "So, you don't think people can change."

He lifted his chin. "I think people make choices in life, and they have to suffer the consequences."

Dean cleared his throat. "Does that go for you too, Bryson?"

Bryson aimed his gun at Dean.

"Wait, Bryson. You didn't tell me how you poisoned Louie. And how in the world did he end up at Weenie's house?"

Bryson grinned. "It's genius. I studied Louie's comings and goings and noticed he would park his truck on some gravel road and then walk through the woods to Weenie's house. I caught him and Donnie Rae getting into an argument after he broke into her house." He cut his eyes at Dean. "Looks like you need to do a better job of serving and protecting the citizens of Harland Creek."

A muscle in Dean's cheek twitched.

"And then what happened?" I tried turning his attention back to me.

Bryson looked at me and smiled. "Louie had a habit of going to the donut shop every morning at a certain time. He would order five donuts and black coffee. I was waiting for him there. I had already ordered my coffee and was grabbing some napkins to go. Louie made some smart comment about cops under his breath. He looked away when Felicia Dantry walked in, and I took that moment to switch coffees with him. You see, I had been doctoring my coffee with that pesticide every morning waiting for him to come in. That afternoon was the last of the poison I had. As luck would have it, he took the coffee, along with his donuts, and left. I followed him to the gravel road and watched as he trotted through the woods to Weenie's house, sipping the coffee as he went. By the time he got to Weenie's house, I could tell he was having difficulty breathing. When he went inside, he only made it to the kitchen island before he collapsed. Before he died, I walked in and smiled at him as he died."

I shivered. How had I been so easily fooled by Bryson?

Bryson chuckled. "I had even called the quilt shop and left that message the day of the snowstorm."

I frowned. "She knows too much. You said that? Why?"

Bryson shrugged. "Just in case the police couldn't figure out it was Skipper. I figured it would put the heat on Weenie since it was her house he died in."

My blood ran cold in my veins. "You planted Skipper's gloves as evidence. That's what you were doing at Weenie's house."

Bryson smirked. "You're not as dumb as I thought you were, Dove."

"Did you give Skipper something? He's not acting right." Dean called out.

Bryson turned his attention back to him and nodded. "Just a little something to help mellow him out. I was going to make it look like he escaped and then shoot him. But since everyone decided to ruin my plan, I guess I'm going with Plan B."

Sloan cocked his head. "What's Plan B?"

Bryson smiled and turned his gun toward me. "I'm taking

Dove hostage and getting out of town. If you follow me, then I'll shoot her."

Dean's murderous look made my heart thud in my chest. He took a step forward.

"Stop, Dean." I shouted. "I'll go with Bryson as long as he leaves Skipper here."

Bryson shoved Skipper to the ground. "That's a deal." He aimed his gun at me. "I'm walking to you, and we'll take your car."

"Dove," Dean warned.

I looked at him and nodded. "It's okay, Dean. It's going to be okay."

I held my hands up and waited as Bryson slowly made his way over while aiming his gun at Dean.

"Want me to take a shot, Dean?" Sloan asked.

Dean shook his head.

When Bryson got within arm's length of me, he pulled me roughly in front of him. He aimed his gun at my head. "Now if anyone tries to follow us, I'll put a bullet in her pretty little head."

He took a step back, and I let out a yell.

"Tarzan!"

The German shepherd growled and latched onto Bryson's butt, pulling him down to the ground. Screaming in pain, Bryson twisted and aimed his gun toward the dog.

Petunia appeared out of nowhere and headed-butted him so hard that it knocked the gun out of his hand. I kicked the gun out of his reach, and the police department descended on him like a swarm of ants.

Once Bryson was handcuffed, Dean gave Tarzan a command. "Release!"

The dog obediently let go and sat while barking at the suspect.

Dean reached for me and pulled me into his arms. He cradled my head between his hands. "Are you okay, Dove?"

I nodded. "Thanks to Tarzan and Petunia."

He grinned and looked at the two animals. "Thanks for the help, guys."

Tarzan gave a toothy grin, and Petunia let out a bleat, then gave Tarzan a lick on the nose.

Bertha and the rest of the quilting ladies finally stepped from around the building and looked at what was going on.

"You got him! That's great!" Maggie nodded. She gave me a sheepish grin. "We were waiting until you gave us the go-ahead to come help, Dove."

Weenie blinked behind her large glasses. "That's not what you said, Maggie. You said you don't have time to get shot today because you have a full calendar tomorrow."

Maggie's face went red.

Sylvia stepped up and wrapped her arm around her business partner. "You must understand, Dove. We need to make up for being closed for so many days."

Bertha snorted. "Those two are petrified of guns. That's why they didn't come running to help."

Weenie blinked. "So why didn't you come help Dove, Bertha?"

Bertha cleared her throat and shifted her weight. "Well, I have this bunion on my foot. Can't run so fast, you see. It's a medical condition."

Mom pushed through the ladies. "Dove, you're okay!" She pulled me into a hug. "Agnes held me back and wouldn't let me follow you."

Elizabeth and Agnes appeared behind Mom. I gave the ladies a smile. "I'm glad they did. You didn't need to see all this."

Lorraine wrapped her arm around Weenie. "Bryson killed Louie. I never would have suspected."

Weenie blinked. "Me either. I guess I'm not a very good judge of character."

I walked over to Weenie and took her hands in mine. "I think you have a big heart, Weenie. And I think we need more like you in the world."

Dean walked over. "Just so it's clear, Weenie, you are no longer a suspect in Louie's murder."

She blinked. "Did you really think I could have done it?"

He cocked his head. "I guess you didn't realize we took your pie as evidence from the crime scene. It did look a bit suspicious that the autopsy said he was poisoned, and he was known for stealing your pies. Of course, it came back negative, and I never really thought you would have killed him. But I have tasted your pies. They're the best in Harland Creek. That alone was motive enough for me." He gave her a teasing grin.

She blushed and smiled. "Thanks, Dean. You know I must have scared Dove when I told her Louie shouldn't have touched my pies. To be honest, I thought God had struck him dead, and that's why I said it."

Dean grinned and walked over to assist his police officers.

As the police took Bryson into custody and the ambulance arrived for Skipper, we all breathed a sigh of relief that one more murder was solved, and Weenie was free and clear.

CHAPTER 34

$\mathcal{I}$ sipped my coffee and looked at Mom over the top the newspaper. It had been a month since Bryson had been arrested for the murder of Louie, and things had finally settled down.

The charges were dropped against Donnie Rae. Mrs. Simpson said she wasn't some helpless old woman and could take care of herself. She'd also taken Donnie Rae under her wing and hired him to be her handyman around her house. It was better money, and she even threw in a meal. He planned on going back to college and starting night classes in the fall.

There was even a happy update with Skipper. His daughter had seen the events on the news and reached out to him. They were set to meet up in a couple of weeks. He was so thrilled that he even talked to Dean about a change in career. Skipper wanted to become a lawyer to help innocent people in jail. Dean connected him with the right people, and he was applying for financial aid.

Linda, on the other hand, was still as ornery as a bull. She liked her life in the Chateau RV Park and didn't want to give up hunting for squirrels. As luck would have it, the new owner of the RV Park didn't raise the rent, so Linda was at least grateful for that.

After the whole case was solved, we held a large party for Weenie and invited Petunia and Tarzan as well. She was grateful things were back to normal and settled back into her old routine of quilting, knitting, and baking pies.

As I sat at the kitchen table, I sighed contently.

"Guess what?" I asked.

Mom stirred sugar and cream into her coffee. "What, dear?"

I bit my lip. "I saw on social media last night that Polly is writing a book about a goat that goes on a trip. She's marketing it to a younger audience and so far, there's been a lot of interest. She even went over to Elizabeth's house to get Petunia's hoof print so she can put it in the book. Isn't that great!"

Mom's eyebrows shot up. "So she's making Petunia famous! That's amazing."

I nodded. "I wonder why Petunia left in the first place. You know, Elizabeth has said that since Petunia came home, she's been staying close and not wanting to leave the house. Do you think she was scared on her adventure?"

Mom laughed and shook her head. "No. I think Petunia wanted to see if the grass was greener on the other side. Turns out it wasn't. While she might have had fun making friends, she prefers her old life of quilting and mysteries."

I sat back in my chair and sipped my coffee. "I think you're right. Sometimes the simple things in life and at home are the best."

ABOUT THE AUTHOR

Jodi Allen Brice is a USA Today best-selling author of over forty novels. She writes several genres including cozy mysteries, women's fiction, and small town romance. She also writes paranormal romance under a different pen name. You can find out more about her books by visiting her website at http://jodiallenbrice.com

While you are there, don't forget to sign up for her newsletter!

Stand alone novels.

So This Is Goodbye

Not Like the Other Girls

Harland Creek Cozy Mystery Quilters

Mystery of the Tea Cup Quilt

The Mystery of the Drunkards Path

The Mystery of the Exploding Heart

The Mystery of the Log Cabin

Harland Creek Cozy Mystery Quilters

Mystery of the Tea Cup Quilt

The Mystery of the Drunkards Path

The Mystery of the Exploding Heart

The Mystery of the Log Cabin

The Mystery of the Crazy Quilt

Tiny Homes and Happy Tails Series

The Journey That Never Ends

The Journey of a Lifetime

Harland Creek Series

Promise Kept

Promise Made

Promise Forever

Christmas in Harland Creek

Promise of Grace

Promise of Hope

Promise of Love

Candy Cane Christmas

Promise of A Hero

Laurel Cove Series
Lakehouse Promises
Lakehouse Secrets
Lakehouse Dreams
Lakehouse Christmas

Stand alone novels.
So This Is Goodbye
Not Like the Other Girls